D0883221

MOLLY AND THE CONFIDENCE MAN

STEPHEN OVERHOLSER

DOUBLEDAY & COMPANY, INC.

GARDEN CITY, NEW YORK

1975

The characters in this book are fictitious,
and any resemblance to actual persons,
living or dead, is purely coincidental.

Library of Congress Cataloging in Publication Data

Overholser, Stephen.
    Molly and the confidence man.

    I. Title.
PZ4.0942Mo   [PS3565.V43]   813'.5'4
ISBN 0-385-04706-1
Library of Congress Catalog Card Number 74–33737

To my mother

MOLLY AND THE
CONFIDENCE MAN

Chapter I

The day before his murder, Chick Owens wrote a letter to his sister, Molly:

Circle 7 Ranch
Liberty, Colorado
June 3, 1892

Dear Sis,

It sure seems funny sending this letter all the way back to New York City when you are probably somewhere out here in the West, investigating one thing or another. When are you going to settle down and get married like other women? Last time you wrote you were somewhere in Texas with another Fenton investigator, tracking a man who had run off with some bank money. How did that come out? Did you catch him? I hope so.

You asked in your letter why I kept on working for the Circle 7 when there was trouble a-brewing. Well, you know us Owens don't run off from trouble, Molly. Also, as I have probably wrote you before, the Circle 7 is owned by a woman named Bess Tanner, and she surely has been good to me in the time I have been riding for her, so I reckon I should stick, come what may. Anyway, she will be needing my testimony next week. Old Justin Dundee, owner of the neighboring ranch, is bringing charges against Bess, and I am going to testify about a JD hide that was found draped over Bess's corral a while back, and also about some JD riders I seen yank down one of their own fences last winter. I believe we can win this case old man Dundee is trumping up against Bess. If we do, I can tell you it will be big news in these parts. Dundee has always had his way around here.

Why don't you head up this way, Molly? Haven't seen you for over two years. That is too long, seeing as we are the last of the Owens of Martin County, Pennsylvania. Besides, I believe some of your work with the Fenton Investigative Agency is too dangerous for a woman, even one as onery as you, and if you came up to this part of the country, you would surely like it and probably stay around. I know you would like Bess. She is onery like you, only some older. Also, there is a certain young lady in Liberty I would like to introduce you to. Why don't you listen to your baby brother for a change and climb on the train and come up here? Liberty is end-of-steel now, and quite a boom town.

Well, take care, Molly. Love always,

Chick

PS. Say, Molly, did you hear the story about what happened when the new schoolmarm wandered into a pasture with a breeding bull, and a cyclone come through? Well, pay me a visit, and I'll tell it to you, Molly.

Chick

Not long after Chick mailed his letter, Molly Owens was in the mining camp of Silverthorne, Colorado. She was there on business. The mining camp was high in the southern Colorado Rockies, some three hundred miles south and east of Liberty. If Chick thought Liberty was a boom town, he should have seen Silverthorne that summer.

In the single, wheel-rutted street of Silverthorne, Molly stood at the edge of a crowd of miners. Among the drunk and sober alike, expectation and excitement ran high. They had gathered to watch a confidence man named Charley Castle. He was preparing to sell bottles of liquid soap at five dollars each. Many of the small bottles would be wrapped in one-hundred-and fifty-dollar bills.

Excitement ran high in Molly, too. But hers was not for the thrill of gambling. As she watched the full-bearded, well-dressed confidence man, a wild idea came to her.

Chapter II

Silverthorne was a new, booming camp. It had sprung up on the strength of a large silver discovery that had been made in '91 near the summit of Silverthorne Mountain. The big mine was close to timberline, 11,000 feet in elevation.

The camp in the narrow valley below the Silverthorne Mine was little more than a random collection of white canvas tents, tar-paper shacks, and three false-fronted frame buildings. Two of these were saloons; the third was a boardinghouse.

The silver strike was so rich that it had become almost instantly legendary. Hard-rock miners, skilled men and novices alike, flocked to Silverthorne like birds to grain. Switchback roads soon laced the mountains. Silverthorne and surrounding mountainsides were pock-marked with prospect holes and tunnels within a few months of the news of the first strike. Most of these were small operations, amounting to two or three men with picks and shovels and big ideas.

When winter broke in '92, the miners returned to the high country around Silverthorne, more this year than before. Stories of huge underground deposits of pure silver were told and retold. But it soon became apparent that history was likely to repeat: Of the men who struck it rich, few were miners. Those who had a sure thing were the shopkeepers, freighters, saloon owners, and madams of Silverthorne. And Charley Castle.

Charley Castle's deep voice lashed out into the evening air like thunder in a storm:

"Wake up! Wake up, and listen to me, you dreamers! The hour has come! We must face the question of the hour! This question I put to you: Gentlemen, how are you fixed for soap?"

Amid the murmurs and chuckles from the crowd of soiled

miners, Molly Owens watched the smooth-talking confidence man, her mind still afire with the wild idea that had come to her. Never before had she violated her instructions, and the thought of doing so now both excited and frightened her.

Charley Castle held a questioning expression on his face like a Shakespearean actor. He stood upon a small box. This height advantage of a few inches gave him command of the crowd. Every man there watched him intently as he raised his arms high and asked in a booming voice:

"What? Have you nothing to say? Do I embarrass you? To be honest, gentlemen, you all look as though you have need of soap." He paused and sniffed the air dramatically. "Gentlemen, I sense your need."

When the tide of the men's laughter subsided, Charley Castle went on speaking in a lower tone of voice, a tone of voice he surely reserved for his close friends. "Gentlemen, I come to you with a message of hope and a message of soap. Today, to meet your great need, I bring a new soap, a wondrous product derived from imported coconut oil. Yes, my friends, coconut oil. This oil is one of the great healing medicines known to modern science. Ask a doctor. Any reputable man of science will bear out the truth of what I say. My new wonder soap is the finest cleansing product on the face of God's earth, gentlemen. It is a true wonder of science."

Charley Castle paused and surveyed his audience. He stood behind a large samples case that was set on a tripod. Now he reached into his samples case and brought out a small bottle filled with green liquid.

"Liquid soap, gentlemen," Charley Castle said, holding the little bottle as though it were a gem, and a fragile one. "The twentieth century dawns before our very eyes! I guarantee you that what this soap won't do for you isn't worth having done. Are you growing bald? Is your hair turning gray? Gentlemen, use my coconut-oil soap, and youthful locks will once again adorn your scalps. You have my guarantee."

Charley Castle's voice dropped to an intimate whisper when he asked, "Are you kept awake nights with a guilty conscience? Use my soap and wash your sins away. Sleep the sleep of innocence!"

He surveyed the crowd once again. The miners were bunched together, watching him with anticipation. Charley Castle's eyes passed over Molly Owens and returned for an instant before moving on. The woman he saw was straw-haired and fair, wearing a long, full dress that buttoned tight at the neck. A lady in a mining camp was worth a second look.

Molly felt Charley Castle's eyes briefly meet hers. She was aware that she was the only woman in the crowd. She wondered what Charley Castle thought of that. If he wasn't surprised by her presence now, she thought, he would be before the end of the evening.

Like a warm, comforting wind, Charley Castle's voice washed over the members of the audience: "Any man among you who wishes to purchase my new wonder soap may now do so. Each bottle sells for fifty cents, and a bargain it is, gentlemen, when you consider the months of research I put into the invention of this product in my own laboratories."

This announcement brought no response from the miners. They watched Charley Castle, waiting for him to go on.

"None among you wants a bargain? All right, gentlemen, perhaps you would rather court the goddess of luck. Perhaps some of you believe the feel of greenbacks is nearer paradise than mere cleanliness. Well, step up, my friends, and watch me closely."

Charley Castle drew out a bulging wallet from his inside coat pocket. As he pulled back his lapel, Molly noticed the gleaming white handle of a small revolver in a shoulder holster.

The wallet bulged with greenbacks. Some were of high denomination—hundreds and fifties—and many were one- and two-dollar bills. Charley Castle stacked the bills on the front edge of his samples case, then replaced the wallet in his inside coat pocket. This move was slightly deliberate, and as the gleaming handle of the revolver flashed like a light,

Molly realized the sight of the weapon was anything but accidental. All the men had probably seen it. Every move in Charley Castle's act, Molly believed, was planned for an effect.

While speaking easily about the state of the nation and the coming twentieth century, Charley Castle swiftly wrapped his bottles of soap in sheets of dark blue wrapping paper. He wrapped every other or every third bottle with a greenback before covering it with wrapping paper. When he did this with a hundred-dollar bill, a deep sound came from the crowd, like a moan or a gasp. Each bottle of soap, when wrapped, was carelessly tossed into the samples case. Though the wrapping was done quickly and with apparent ease, Molly noticed Charley Castle's brow was shining with sweat.

The last bottle was wrapped, slowly, with a one-hundred-dollar bill.

"Now, gentlemen," Charley Castle said, "for those of you with sporting blood, I offer a bottle of liquid soap for the price of five dollars."

Charley Castle paused. Again Molly felt his eyes sweep past hers.

"But first," he went on, "to show you what kind of man I am, let me make this offer: If any man among you will show me a ten-dollar bill, I'll give him a ten. That's right; you heard me right. A ten for a ten. Who can show me a ten? Just wave it over your head. I make this offer only once, and only to prove what a generous man I am. Well?"

None of the miners moved or spoke. They watched Charley Castle, knowing that no sane man would give a ten-dollar bill away, yet they wondered what his game was. Each waited for another to take the bait. Their attention, Molly noticed, had been fixed on the bottles in the samples case, but now they watched Charley Castle intently.

"So," Charley Castle said sadly, "not a man here has sporting blood in his veins, after all."

In answer to this challenge a bull-necked miner wearing a dirty mackinaw and a wool cap spoke up: "Aw, hell, I got a ten." He held a ten-dollar bill over his head and waved it. "Let me see yours, mister. Hand it over."

Charley Castle smiled and reached into his vest pocket. He pulled out a dime and said, "Here you are, my friend. You called my bluff. A ten for a ten was the bargain. I'm the loser and I seek no sympathy."

Harsh laughter and whoops of derision burst from the crowd. Charley Castle tossed the dime to the man. He had looked defiant a moment ago; now he looked sheepish.

"Gentlemen," Charley Castle said to the smiling crowd, "who among you is a gambling man?" He set half a dozen wrapped bottles of soap on the front edge of his samples case. "Take the bottle of your choice for five dollars, gentlemen."

A miner with one thumb thrust jauntily through his red suspenders, still grinning from the joke that had been played, said, "I been watching that last one you wrapped up, Charley. It was wrapped in a hunnert. It's that one right there."

Charley Castle took the miner's five-dollar gold piece and allowed him to select the bottle he thought he'd seen wrapped in a hundred-dollar bill. The men close to the miner pressed around him and watched as he tore away the blue wrapping paper.

The miner had been wrong, but not all wrong. The little bottle was wrapped in a fifty-dollar bill. The sight of it, as the jubilant miner waved it over his head, brought the crowd surging forward, thrusting five-dollar bills and gold pieces at Charley Castle.

For nearly half an hour Molly watched men elbow their way up to Charley Castle, trade five dollars for a small blue package, then come back out of the crowd, tearing at their purchases. A few men got twenties and tens, but most were one- or two-dollar bills, or blanks.

When the pace of buying slackened, another fifty-dollar bill was discovered, and the lucky miner let out a whoop. This brought the crowd rushing back to Charley Castle like ants to spilled honey. Many men bought bottles of soap for second and third times, thinking they would increase the odds of drawing a hundred dollars or at least fifty.

Before Molly left the crowd to walk back up the street, she heard some of the men grumbling at their losses. The miner who had won the first fifty-dollar bill confessed that he had put half back into Charley Castle's hand.

"Well," he concluded, "at least I skinned him for twenty-five."

"That's better than I done," another hard-rock miner said. "He stung me twice. All I got out of it was a one."

"Charley sure stung me," a third added. With respect, he said, "Ain't he a slick one?"

Later in the evening the crowd had dwindled to a dozen onlookers. On the ground around them, blue wrapping papers were trampled into the dirt like crumpled hopes. Charley Castle lifted his samples case off the tripod and showed its empty insides to anyone who was interested in looking.

"Gentlemen, I'm sold out," Charley Castle said. "I'll have to return to my laboratories and replenish my supply."

"Say, Charley," one of the remaining observers said, "whatever happened to those soap bottles you wrapped in hundreds?"

Another miner, shaggy and bearded, echoed, "Yeah, what did happen to 'em?"

In the gathering darkness Charley Castle had stepped off his small box. He picked the box up and set it inside his samples case along with the collapsible tripod. He answered the man casually:

"Some lucky souls purchased those bottles for five dollars."

The first man who had spoken persisted, "Well, I never saw them."

Charley Castle said, "The lucky winners undoubtedly have their reasons for not boasting of their good fortune."

"I don't get you," the man said.

"Why, if you made a big strike," Charley Castle said, "would you be telling the world about it?"

"No, I reckon I wouldn't," the man conceded.

The shaggy man laughed as he saw the implication of Charley Castle's question. "I wouldn't, either. Around this camp some joker would likely take it away from me."

Charley Castle nodded, picked up his samples case, and bid the remaining men good night. He walked up the narrow street, passing a row of white tents that glowed now from lanterns inside. As he approached one of the false-fronted saloons farther up the street, he heard a man inside singing sourly:

"Old Dan Tucker was a fine old man,
  He washed his face in a frying pan;
  He combed his hair with a wagon wheel,
  And died with a toothache in his heel."

Smiling, Charley Castle walked through the long rectangle of yellow light that streamed out of the open door of the saloon. Another man inside took up the song, and sang it better:

"Old Dan Tucker's mother-in-law
  Was the ugliest thing I ever saw;
  Her eyes stuck out and her nose stuck in,
  Her upper lip hung over her chin."

Charley Castle walked on to the frame boardinghouse. He knew other verses to the Dan Tucker song, more colorful than those two, and he would have liked to have gone into the saloon and joined in the singing. But he had learned long ago not to have business and pleasure in the same town. Some of the evening's losers might be using a bottle to nurse a grudge. Early in the morning, before sunup, Charley Castle would leave Silverthorne. He would seek his pleasure and relaxation in another town.

That, at least, was his plan. Entering the big boardinghouse, he mounted the steps to his room on the second floor. He walked down the long hallway amid the smells and snores of sleeping miners.

Charley Castle unlocked his door. As he entered the tiny room, he reached into his vest pocket for a match. At the moment he struck the match, he felt a small circle of cold steel pressed against the bare skin below his ear.

"One move, Charley Castle," he heard a woman say, "and I'll blow your head open."

Chapter III

Molly thumbed the hammer of her derringer back to full cock. Charley Castle felt the small *click* ring through his skull like a blow.

"Look what civilization has come to now," Charley Castle said.

Molly reached around him and brought out the pearl-handled revolver from his shoulder holster. She backed away and told him to light the lamp. A coal-oil lamp with a badly smoked chimney was on a table beside the bed. After lighting it, Charley Castle slowly turned and faced his intruder. He studied her for a long moment, then said:

"I've seen you before."

Molly nodded. Her heart raced with excitement.

"Yes, I remember you," Charley Castle said. "You watched my act tonight."

Molly nodded again.

"You were watching me like you had my act figured out."

"No," Molly said, "you're too fast."

Charley Castle took that as a compliment and grinned. But when he glanced at the two guns Molly had aimed at him, he said soberly, "So you've come to relieve me of my take."

"No, I haven't," Molly said.

"Then you've come to kill me."

Molly asked, "Do you have enemies like that?"

Charley Castle nodded. "Poor losers."

"I'm not one of them," Molly said.

"I'd remember you if you were," Charley Castle said. "You're probably a relative of one." He paused and asked, "You're not one of those Greers out of Montana, are you?"

"You have the wrong idea about me," Molly said. "I'm not here to rob you or kill you."

Charley Castle smiled ruefully and shook his head. "Reading people's faces is my life's work. You're a lovely young woman, but I can see you're a woman with a mission."

"You're right about that," Molly said. "But you're wrong about my mission, as you call it. My name is Molly Owens. I'm an operative for the Fenton Investigative Agency. I'm here to serve you with a warrant for your arrest."

Charley Castle was surprised. "Well, look what civilization has come to now. Come to think of it, I did hear that the Pinkertons were using women nowadays."

Molly said, "The Fenton Agency is Pinkerton's biggest competitor."

"Too bad a pretty lady like you couldn't find honest work," Charley Castle said. "What are you arresting me for?"

"The warrant is from Topeka," Molly said. "You can read it later. Right now we're leaving."

"Leaving?" Charley Castle said. With his hands outstretched, he advanced a step closer to Molly. He demanded an explanation.

Molly raised the derringer and took deliberate aim at his chest. Charley Castle retreated.

"There's something we'd better get understood right now," she said. "You're my prisoner. I'm taking you back to Topeka whether you like it or not. I'll handcuff you if I have to. Try to escape, and I'll shoot you."

"You're a hard woman," Charley Castle said.

"Now we understand one another," Molly said.

"Wait," Charley Castle protested, "I don't know what I'm wanted for in Topeka. I've never even been in that town. You've got the wrong man."

"You can explain your innocence to the judge," Molly said. "Get your bag and come on. I have a buggy waiting."

Charley Castle glared at her. Then he must have decided further protestations would be futile, for he gathered up his belongings and tossed them into a carpetbag. He snatched up the bag in one hand and angrily grabbed the samples case with the other. He traveled light, Molly noticed. She trained her derringer on him and gave him a wide berth as he passed by on his way out the door. She blew out the lamp and followed him out of the room and down the hallway.

They crossed Silverthorne's darkened street to the livery stable. Blaring sounds, singing men mostly, came from the open door of the nearby saloon. In front of the livery a one-horse buggy was tied at the rail. Molly climbed up to the seat. She advised Charley Castle to do the same. He growled once, then tossed his bag and samples case beneath the seat, and climbed up. Molly handed him the reins.

Charley Castle drove the buggy down the rutted street. Molly held her derringer in her hand and watched him carefully. She did not know if he had friends or accomplices in town. She doubted it, but she wanted to be sure he did not try to signal anyone. The loud sounds of singing and yelling and the few lights of the mining camp fell behind as they followed the road that led down a canyon and into the darkness ahead.

The moon rose an hour before midnight. On the high, jagged horizon it was a pale orange disc, the color of reflected fire. Within an hour the moon had risen higher, grown smaller, and turned white as frost. Now its light cast shadows deep into the pine forest along the road. The canyon road was a good one. It had been built to carry heavy freight and ore wagons. The road wound its way out of the canyon and into the foothills. Eventually it would lead to Colorado's eastern grassy plains, and on to the rail line.

Charley Castle had maintained a heavy silence since leaving Silverthorne. Molly had not expected this behavior. She had thought of him as a man of words, a windy talker who could argue his way out of any corner. Molly's mental picture of him had been largely formed by the written report on Charley Castle's background that had accompanied her instructions from the Fenton home office. And after seeing his soap game and first meeting him in his room, her mental picture was confirmed. He was a talker.

Molly had heard of Charley Castle before she read the

Fenton report. Most folks had. His reputation was widespread throughout the country, particularly in the western states. Charley Castle was considered to be one of the two or three best confidence men and sleight-of-hand artists alive. In the Fenton report Molly learned that he had become so famous and recognizable that the larger gambling casinos in the West would not let him in the door, much less touch a deck of cards.

Charley Castle had used many different games in his career, from card and dice games to the pea game. His soap game was a recent invention, but had quickly become famous and was described in the Fenton report as his "masterpiece of deception."

Castle was no thief. He had never spent a day in prison. He had spent some time in city jails, but these short stays ended as soon as he agreed to pay an exorbitant "fee" to the local city marshal or mayor for a salesman's license. Charley Castle apparently had a great dislike for these licenses. He had often risked arrest to avoid paying for them.

Charley Castle had no record of violent behavior or even of public drunkenness. His reputation, as outlined in the Fenton report, was that of a gentleman. He was often seen in the company of respected women when he was not "working."

Molly Owens was in New Mexico when she received her assignment and the background report on Charley Castle. Her imagination was caught by the description of this unusual man. And she was fascinated with the idea of capturing him.

Molly had been working with another Fenton operative on behalf of a Santa Fe bank. They were investigating a large land sale. During the field work, the operative, a fleshy, complaining man whom Molly disliked, was thrown from his horse. He claimed to have suffered a severe back sprain. Molly happily completed the investigation alone, filed her report with the Santa Fe bank, and sent a duplicate copy to New York City.

By return mail she received the report on Charley Castle. A warrant was out for him. The mayor of Topeka, Kansas, at his own expense, had engaged the Fenton Investigative

Agency to locate Charley Castle and return him to Topeka for prosecution. Castle, the report said, was believed to be in southern Colorado, or possibly Denver.

Molly was instructed to travel by train from Santa Fe to Denver, stopping in the larger towns along the way to ask for information regarding Charley Castle's whereabouts. Under no circumstances was she to venture out alone to capture him. This was against company policy. She was to continue on to Denver, whether she had located Castle or not, and take a room in the Brown Palace Hotel. There she would meet with another Fenton operative, a man named Clarence Hoffman. He, too, was headed for Denver with similar instructions.

At the Brown Palace Hotel, Molly and Clarence Hoffman were to compare notes, then set out together to find and capture Castle. Molly was discouraged with these orders. Clarence Hoffman would very likely turn out to be another soft, ineffective investigator who alternately complained and gave senseless instructions. Molly wished she could be given a chance to complete this assignment on her own. She was convinced she could handle it.

There was a pleasant footnote to the instructions, however. Her accumulated mail would be forwarded to the Brown Palace Hotel. She hadn't received a single letter for over a month.

Molly took a northbound train from Santa Fe to a mining and mill town in southern Colorado called Gold Run. Charley Castle was not there, but his reputation was. Molly picked up no solid information until she interviewed a ticket clerk in the railway station. He recalled overhearing a conversation last winter between two gamblers in which one mentioned that Charley Castle was living in Colorado Springs.

Molly found Colorado Springs to be a small town with wide streets, overshadowed by a snow-topped mountain named Pikes Peak. Molly soon learned that her lead from the ticket clerk had been accurate. Charley Castle had wintered in Colorado Springs at the Antlers Hotel. He and a wealthy widow had been in constant company throughout the winter months, and it was commonly rumored they would be married in the spring.

But when the winter's snows melted away, so did Charley Castle.

The trail ended with Castle's disappearance from Colorado Springs. Molly spent two days talking to people around the fancy hotel. She spoke to clerks in stores, newspaper boys, and bench sitters. Molly picked up a great amount of gossip, including one man's solemn belief Charley Castle lived high in the Rockies, in a cave whose walls were lined with pure gold.

During this time Molly learned of the big silver strike on Silverthorne Mountain. And after reading a newspaper account of the booming region, Molly came to her own conclusions about Charley Castle's whereabouts. The tug of her intuition became a strong pull. She would have to go there. It was, she thought, only a small violation of her instructions.

A new railroad station had been built on the line north of Colorado Springs. This station was designed to handle the sudden rush of traffic to the Silverthorne camp. Several businesses had already built up around the station. By paying in advance, Molly was able to rent a buggy there. Over the protests of the liveryman, she drove to Silverthorne alone.

In the evening Molly watched Charley Castle perform his confidence game. She realized she could easily arrest this man herself.

Chapter IV

The mining road dropped out of the foothills. Ahead, by moonlight, Molly saw it stretching out across the plains like a gentle crease in the land.

She felt nearly overcome with fatigue. Yet now more than ever she had to stay awake and alert until they reached the railroad station on the prairie. She was puzzled by Charley Castle's long silence. Her mental picture of him as a silver-tongued man of words was not proving true. Her curiosity was heightened.

"Mr. Castle," Molly said, hoping to engage him in conversation.

Charley Castle stared ahead and said nothing.

"Mr. Castle," Molly said, "perhaps now I can explain some things to you."

Charley Castle kept his silence, looking ahead.

Molly said, "I think I can explain some things about the warrant for your arrest."

When she had decided Charley Castle would not speak to her at all, he said quietly, "Miss Owens, I have nothing to say to you. I told you once you have the wrong man. I haven't been in Topeka, Kansas, for years."

"I thought you said you'd never been there."

"Well, it has been so long that it might as well have been never," he said.

Molly smiled. She *had* expected him to be quick-witted. "I'm sure you'll be able to explain everything, Mr. Castle, when you get back to Topeka."

"I'll call you for a character witness at my trial," he said.

Happy that he was responding even sarcastically to her conversation, she asked, "Don't you want to know what the charges against you are?"

"No."

"Why?" she asked.

"They're false," Charley Castle said.

"That's the only reason you don't want to know?" Another reason had occurred to her.

Charley Castle made no reply.

Molly said, "You're not thinking that you will never have to face a judge in Topeka, are you? You're not thinking about escaping?"

"Now, what on God's earth would give me an idea like that?" he asked.

Molly ignored his sarcasm. "Don't try it," she said.

"Thanks for the advice."

"You're welcome," Molly said.

Charley Castle suddenly turned to her. "You're a pushy woman, Miss Owens, mighty pushy."

Molly felt a sudden rush of anger. "And you don't know how to handle women like me, do you?"

"It's a man's world, Miss Owens," Charley Castle said.

"Is that why you went off and left that widow?" she asked.

In the moonlight Molly saw his glare, and felt it. "What are you talking about?"

"That widow you left in Colorado Springs," Molly said. "It's the talk of the town."

"I'll bet it is," Charley Castle growled. "I suppose you asked everybody in town about me."

"Just about," Molly said.

Charley Castle looked ahead and said, "Whatever happened to a man's privacy?"

"He never had it," Molly said.

Charley Castle returned to his silence. Molly soon lost satisfaction with her verbal victory. She realized it would be a quiet trip from now on. The distance between the new railroad station and the Silverthorne camp seemed much longer this time. Molly struggled with her own fatigue. It seeped through her like warm water and she yearned to succumb to it. She took a deep breath and straightened up in the buggy seat, peering ahead, straining to see by moonlight what wasn't there.

Then she did see something ahead, a dim but large form that gradually took shape as they approached. Soon Molly recognized the tall water tower that was beside the railroad station.

The row of buildings along the railroad tracks was lighted by the moon. A livery stable and blacksmith shop was on one end of the row, next to the steep-roofed railroad station. On the far end, next to a saloon, was a large warehouse. It was owned by the Silverthorne Mine Company and was used as a supply and storage building.

Molly directed Charley Castle to the corral beside the livery and blacksmith shop. She got out of the buggy stiffly and stretched, watching Charley Castle do the same. She told him to unhook the horse and turn him out in the corral.

He led the tired horse into the corral. After closing the gate and returning, he asked, "Well, what now?"

"We wait," Molly said.

"For what?" he asked. "Or who—a lawman?"

"There is a northbound train due around sunup," she said.

Charley Castle pulled out his pocket watch and read it by moonlight. "You had this little trip planned out to a T, didn't you? It'll be light in an hour." He put his watch away and added, "Now I understand why you were in such a hurry to get me out of Silverthorne. You cut the time pretty thin, didn't you?"

"It worked out all right," Molly said. She motioned to the peak-roofed station building. "Walk around to the front of the station, Mr. Castle. We can sit on the benches there."

Molly followed him around the livery stable to the front of the station. Several benches had been placed there to accommodate waiting passengers. She told Charley Castle to sit at the end of one of the benches and put his hand on the arm of the bench.

"What for?" he asked.

Molly waved her derringer at him. Charley Castle did as he was told. Even though he watched her suspiciously, he did not see what was happening until it was too late. Molly snapped a handcuff on his wrist, the other on the arm of the bench. Charley Castle jerked his hand up, too late.

"Now, you didn't have to do that!" he said.

Molly felt the tension go out of her. She sat on the far end of a bench that was a dozen feet away from Charley Castle. For the first time since leaving Silverthorne, she could relax.

"You don't have to put me in irons!" Charley Castle said angrily. "Where do you think I'd run off to, anyway?"

"Nowhere, now," Molly said.

"There's no place to go out here," he said. "We're in the middle of nowhere."

"There are horses here," Molly said.

Charley Castle said indignantly, "I'm no horse thief!"

"Oh, I'm sure you'd leave some money behind," Molly said.

"You plain don't trust me, do you?" Charley Castle said.

Molly realized her eyes were closed. "Right now I do."

"Take me out of these irons," Charley Castle said. His anger was smoldering and he spoke in a low voice. "I won't be treated like a common criminal. I won't be hauled off in irons—especially not by any woman."

Molly swung her feet up on the bench and stretched out, trying to find the least uncomfortable position on the hard bench.

"Take me out of these irons," Charley Castle said again.

To Molly, his voice was growing far away.

"Listen," Charley Castle said, "I'll give you my word I won't try to escape. You can sleep all you want, and I'll be here when you wake up. You have my word. What more do you want?"

Molly remembered wondering if she should reply and prolong the argument, but that was the last thing she remembered. She jerked awake to a bright sky and the sudden knowledge that something was terribly wrong.

In the light of day she looked at Charley Castle. He still sat on the end of the bench, apparently asleep. Molly thought he looked comfortable, and she was slow in understanding why his arms should not be folded across his chest.

Molly smelled wood smoke in the air, then heard a stove lid clang inside the station house. *The stationmaster must be starting his breakfast,* she thought. Molly sat up and looked in her handbag. She found her loaded derringer, Charley Castle's pearl-handled revolver, and the pair of handcuffs she had put on him last night.

Molly looked up in surprise and alarm. Her eyes met Charley Castle's. He laughed.

"I told you I wouldn't run off," he said. "I'm a man of my word."

Molly stared at him, unable to speak.

Charley Castle pointed to the legs of the bench he sat on. "These benches aren't bolted down, Miss Owens. As soon as you started snoring, I slid this bench over to you and dug your keys out of your handbag. I gave those damned irons back to you. Now, don't go snapping them back on me. I won't have you humiliating me."

Molly stood and turned away from him. Her face was hot. She was ashamed of her own stupidity, and frightened, too. Had her prisoner been a man of different character, she would be dead now.

As that terrifying thought passed through her mind, she felt a great sense of relief and a strong urge to thank Charley Castle. But how could she thank him for being the man he was? She knew she couldn't. And she knew, too, that their relationship had changed, perhaps had even reversed. Charley Castle was still her prisoner, but now it was by virtue of his consent, of his *word,* that he would not escape.

Molly wondered how she would cope with this relationship. Her past experiences with prisoners would be of no help. She felt foolish now at her rash decision to capture a man like Charley Castle by herself.

Molly took a deep breath and turned to face him, expecting him to laugh again. But Charley Castle's legs were stretched out in front of him, his arms were folded across his chest again, and his eyes were closed.

Far to the south Molly heard the shrill whistle of an approaching steam engine. On the flat horizon to the east, the sun was up.

Chapter V

The grassy prairie of eastern Colorado rolled past the windows of the train's passenger coach. Charley Castle stared out of one of these windows. In the seat beside him Molly listened to the sounds of the wheels as they clicked monotonously over the rails.

They sat near the back of the passenger coach. It was more

than half filled with the usual variety of travelers—a few drummers, women with restless children, cowboys, a young couple across the aisle who might have been newlyweds, and several well-dressed businessmen.

Molly still felt ashamed of her act of stupidity back at the station, but now she was less troubled by it. It was behind her. The worst had not happened. And it required little thought for her to imagine herself bound by her own handcuffs back there behind the livery, gagged with her own scarf, and Charley Castle traveling away on the northbound train, laughing.

But that had not happened. And now Denver was ahead.

The more Molly thought about Charley Castle, and the enigmatic man he was, the more curious she became. He was a man whose appearance alone was impressive and memorable. His full beard was trimmed. The expression in his eyes was both thoughtful and amused, as though life was a complicated game and he carried the only rule book.

But he had something else, Molly realized. Charley Castle had *presence*. He was a man people turned to watch as he passed by. Molly had observed that even as they boarded the train and walked down the aisle of the passenger coach. People had turned to look at him, not her. Charley Castle appeared to Molly to be a man who took this gift of presence for granted, never doubting he had it. He used his gift, and profited from it.

So far the only real insight Molly had had into Charley Castle's personality was his vehement objection to being handcuffed and treated as a common criminal. Molly had suspected from the beginning that Castle had a high opinion of himself, but now she realized he was also very conscious of what others thought of him. Being carted off in irons in public view must have been one of his nightmares. She wondered if he had others.

"Mr. Castle," Molly said.

He spoke without turning to face her: "You might as well call me Charley. Everybody else does."

To her, it did not seem right, now. "I'll call you Mr. Castle."

"Suit yourself," he said.

"Mr. Castle, I'm carrying the warrant from Topeka," Molly said. "You may read it now."

"I may?" he asked sarcastically.

"I know you said you weren't interested," Molly said. "But I want to assure you everything is legal."

"How could it be?" Charley Castle asked.

"I mean, the warrant is legal," Molly said, not liking the drift of their conversation.

"That's one worthless piece of paper I'm not interested in," Charley Castle said, looking back out the window.

"I should think you would be," Molly said, "so you will be in a position to answer the charges against you."

Charley Castle said nothing.

"Or I could explain the charges to you," Molly said.

He leaned back in his seat and closed his eyes. "You are determined to do that, aren't you?"

"I think it's only fair that you know what they are," she said.

Charley Castle said, "And it was only fair for you to sneak into my room and shove a gun into my ear, wasn't it?"

Molly felt her face grow warm. "I had to do it that way."

Charley Castle smiled ironically. "Did you think I was a desperado of some kind?"

"I didn't know what you were," Molly said. As an afterthought she added, "I only knew you weren't exactly an honest businessman."

That was the wrong thing to say. Charley Castle straightened up in his seat and threw a furious look at her, like a stone. "You still don't know anything about me, Miss Owens." He slumped back into his seat. After a long silence he asked quietly, "So you think I'm a crook, do you?"

"Ohhhh," Molly said cautiously, "not exactly."

"Not exactly," Charley Castle repeated. "Well, what exactly?"

"You *are* a confidence man," Molly said.

"Now, what does that mean?" Charley Castle asked.

"It means you gain people's confidence," Molly said, "and then you trick them."

"Did I gain your confidence?" he asked.

"No," she said, knowing she was being led. "Not all of it."

"That's right," Charley Castle said. "I didn't gain your confidence because you weren't trying to get something for nothing. Do you remember my act—all of it?"

"I think so," Molly said. "Except the very last. I didn't see that part."

"Because you were busy sneaking into my room so you could waylay me," Charley Castle said. "By the way, how did you get in there? I left that room locked."

Molly said, "The owner let me in."

"For what reason?" Charley Castle asked indignantly.

Molly smiled. "What do you think?"

Charley Castle shook his head. "Now I see why these sneaking investigative agencies are using women. When are you going to find an honest way to make a living?"

"Mr. Castle—"

"All right," he interrupted. "What I wanted to tell you was about the first part of my act—the part you saw. You remember when I made that deal for the ten-dollar bill? A ten for a ten? I always say something like, 'I make this offer to show what a generous man I am.' Well, Miss Owens, does that offer show me up for a generous man?"

Molly shook her head.

"Right there I'm telling folks to keep their money in their pockets. If they don't, then it will go into my pocket. Some men figure that out, some don't. Those who don't, deserve what they get—or lose."

Charley Castle paused and added, "So there's nothing dishonest about my work, Miss Owens. You get that through your head."

Unknowingly, Molly had touched a sore point. She found herself unable to reply and unable to match his stare.

Charley Castle went on, "Now, I don't mind admitting I've done some things in the past that were shady. I used to do some gambling when I was younger. I played cards for several years—in Denver, mostly. I've always been good with my hands, and when I got bored with being honest, I began inventing a few little tricks that kept the odds in my favor. The trouble was, I got too good at it. I never got caught—though some professional gamblers tried hard enough—but I pushed it too far. I made too much money too fast. I was young and didn't know when to lay back. I ended up with a pile of money and a bad reputation. In Denver today I'm lucky if I can get inside a saloon just for a drink.

"It was in Denver that I got to working street corners with a samples case and tripod like any other street hawker. Only, I wasn't selling. I was working the pea game with three walnut shells. That's one game folks never get tired of. They'll play it over and over again because they think they're going to get it figured out. They never do, of course. But that pea game, after I mastered it, was a killer for boredom. I got to hate the thing. What's the use of making money if it isn't any fun? Why, I was ready to quit and go into a regular business of some kind."

The memory made Charley Castle smile. "But that moment of weakness passed and I got to thinking about inventing a new game. I heard about this imported coconut-oil soap. A man in Chicago had a warehouse full of the stuff. He couldn't sell it because people had never heard of it. They didn't trust it. I got to thinking about how I could make coconut-oil soap more desirable. It took me most of a year to think the game out and work up a spiel. And it about killed me to get the hand movements worked out. I still can't do it in daylight. It has to be done in the evening when folks can't see as much as they think they can. The soap game requires a ton of concentration. Everything has to be just so."

He looked at Molly. "There is one thing I want you to remember. I give the people what they want. If I didn't, I wouldn't be in business." Charley Castle leaned back in his seat.

Molly was happy he had taken her into his confidence. It gave her the courage to ask a question. "Mr. Castle, how do you do it?"

Charley Castle laughed. "You're asking for my trade secrets? Well, someday I might show you a thing or two. But not now. I already told you too much."

The train rolled on north and began angling west on its way to Denver. The foothills of the Rocky Mountains were closer now, but the plains out east had changed very little. The prairie had a gentle roll to it, cut here and there by dry washes. The prairie grasses were green and many little flowers were in bloom.

Molly had never been in Denver. She recalled that the ranch where her brother had been working for the past two years was about a hundred miles north and west of Denver. It was a shame to be so close and not be able to see him. Molly knew she wouldn't have time. She wondered if the Circle 7 Ranch was in prairie country like this. Molly thought of Chick, tried to picture him in her mind, and then was brought out of her thoughts when the train slowed.

The train stopped at a water tower on the outskirts of a small coal-mining town. A few of the passengers got out and stretched their legs. Near the front of the coach a baby, awakened by the stop, began to cry and was comforted by its mother.

Charley Castle surprised Molly by turning to her and asking, "Well, when are you going to get around to telling me what the charges against me are in Topeka?"

Molly said, "You made it plain to me you weren't interested."

Charley Castle shrugged, glancing out the window. He looked back at her and said, "This is the last stop before Denver. We have to pass the time somehow."

Molly looked back into his sparkling eyes. She had the distinct feeling he was trying to tell her something, indirectly, as he had described in his spiel about a ten for a ten.

"You talk as though we won't be seeing one another after Denver," Molly said cautiously.

Charley Castle grinned. "I didn't say that at all."

Molly felt more suspicious of him than ever. She could easily recall the details of the warrant. Molly had read the document several times, along with an attached letter from the mayor of Topeka.

"The warrant," she said, "calls for the arrest of one Charles Castle on the charge of gambling in a public place, operating a dishonest gambling device, and misrepresentation."

"Now, what does all that mean?" he asked.

"It means you're a confidence man," Molly said.

"And what crime was I supposed to be committing?" Charley Castle asked.

Remembering the letter attached to the warrant, Molly said, "You were operating the pea game. The mayor of Topeka was in your audience. He thought he understood the game, but, after losing $800, he came to the conclusion that you were operating a dishonest game. He had you arrested and jailed, but you escaped." Molly added, "And you're wanted for jail breaking."

Molly knew, too—but didn't say so—that the whole affair had created great personal embarrassment for the mayor; he had hired, at his own expense, the Fenton Investigative Agency to have Castle located and brought back to Topeka.

"So the mayor sent a woman with a gun after me," he said.

That was not exactly right, but it was an interesting way to sum things up. Molly did not deny it.

Charley Castle muttered, "Look what civilization has come to."

With a long blast of its whistle and a series of jerks and loud *clanks,* the train pulled away. The water tower and the little coal-mining town slid past the windows of the passenger car. The train's wheels began singing their monotonous song. Speaking over it, Molly asked,

"You're innocent of those charges, Mr. Castle?"

"I am," he said.

Molly said, "But the warrant has your name and description."

"My name has been borrowed before," Charley Castle said with a shrug. "That's the price of fame."

Chapter VI

Molly was surprised to find Union Station in Denver crowded with train travelers and well-wishers. Denver still had a reputation as a cow town, but the rushing crowds here matched in size and apparel any she had seen in larger cities. The majority of the men wore stylish dark suits and derbies; the women wore frilly blouses and long skirts. Molly had expected to see only lanky cowboys, farmers, and chunky frontierswomen.

A legless man selling newspapers in front of Union Station recognized Charley Castle and called out his name. "You back in town, Charley?"

Charley Castle walked over to the man's stand and bought a newspaper. The legless man sold tobaccos and assorted curios, too. Charley Castle picked up a fossil and examined it.

"I can make you a good price on that fossil," the legless man said. He pointed to a box on his table. "Take a look at that petrified wood there, Charley. Ain't it purty?"

Charley Castle picked up a chunk. "It is, at that."

"I can make you a good price on it."

Charley Castle smiled and shook his head.

"How's business these days?" the legless man asked.

"Fair," Charley Castle said.

"Folks are saying you're one of the richest men in the state of Colorado nowadays, Charley."

"Don't you believe it," Charley Castle said. "I'm better at spending money than I am at making it."

The legless man laughed. "That's me, too, Charley."

Charley Castle turned to leave.

"You gonna be in Denver a spell?"

Over his shoulder Charley Castle said, "I don't know. I haven't planned that far ahead yet."

The legless man laughed again. "That sounds like you."

Molly and Charley Castle rode in a hired carriage to the Brown Palace Hotel. Molly asked who the legless man was.

Charley Castle said, "I've forgotten his name. He has been selling newspapers from his stand there for years."

"How did he lose his legs?" she asked.

"He was working out in the train yard, coupling and uncoupling freight cars," Charley Castle said. "You only get one mistake in that trade."

The Brown Palace Hotel proclaimed itself to be Denver's newest and finest hotel. Molly could not dispute the claim. It was an impressive building. The floor of the spacious lobby was covered with thick carpeting. Ornate pieces of furniture, the upholstery matching the carpet in color, were evenly distributed across the lobby. Behind the polished desk, a smiling clerk greeted them.

Charley Castle stood silently, and uncomfortably, beside Molly as she paid in advance for two rooms, 406 and 407. Molly asked the clerk if a Clarence Hoffman was registered. He spun the register around and flipped back through the pages, running his finger down each one.

"Ah, yes," the clerk said, stopping his finger near the bottom of a page. "Clarence Hoffman, 319. Do you wish to send him a message?" Anticipating Molly's nod, the clerk handed her a sheet of paper.

Molly lifted the pen from an ink bottle and wrote: "Meet me in 406. Molly Owens."

The clerk rang a bell on his desk, folded the note in half, and handed it to the bellboy who had appeared, Molly thought, from nowhere. The clerk rang his bell a second time. Another bellboy came and picked up Molly's luggage and Charley Castle's carpetbag. He declined the bellboy's offer to carry the samples case. They followed the bellboy into the elevator and rode up to the fourth floor.

In room 406, Molly and Charley Castle waited silently. Charley Castle stood at the window, looking out. The window gave a good view of Denver, overlooking the city's brick and granite buildings and the crosswork of electrical wires that were suspended from poles like thick, black cobwebs.

Molly sat on the bed, thinking that as soon as Clarence Hoffman came the nature of the assignment would change. From here on, the trip to Topeka would be routine. And for the first time Molly thought, *I don't want to do this kind of work for the rest of my life.* She wondered why that thought had come to her now.

She was brought out of her thoughts by a single, loud knock on the door. She opened it to find a tall, broad-shouldered, roughly handsome man standing there, holding a black derby in his hands.

"Miss Molly Owens?"

Molly nodded and started to speak.

"I'm Clarence Hoffman," he said gruffly.

Molly nodded again and asked him in. She smelled whiskey on his breath, and from his gruff manner she realized he had not been looking forward to working on an assignment with a woman. She felt even more discouraged with the trip ahead.

Clarence Hoffman lumbered into the room. He stopped short when he saw Charley Castle. He turned to Molly, confusion clouding his face.

"Who's this?" he demanded.

Molly said casually, "Charley Castle."

Clarence Hoffman's eyes swung from her to Castle, then back again. "You weren't supposed to nab him on your own. Didn't your orders tell you that?"

"Yes," Molly said.

"What are you trying to do?" Clarence Hoffman asked. "Get yourself killed?"

Charley Castle laughed.

"Our paths crossed," Molly said. "The opportunity to capture him was too good to pass up."

Clarence Hoffman shook his head. "You shouldn't have done that. You went against orders."

"Well, it's done," Molly said impatiently. "When do we leave for Topeka?"

Clarence Hoffman clenched his derby in his hands. This woman was trying to make things move too fast for him. "In the morning, I reckon. If I can get tickets." He added, "This is going to be tough to explain to the home office. I was supposed to go after Castle, too."

"I'm the one who'll have to do the explaining," Molly said.

Clarence Hoffman looked at Molly and shook his head again as though she understood nothing. He started to speak, then he glanced at Charley Castle and interrupted himself.

"Say, why ain't he handcuffed?" he demanded. "You trying to get us both killed?" Clarence Hoffman opened his coat and drew a large revolver out of his waistband.

Charley Castle retreated. The weapon was aimed at his face.

Molly shouted, "What are you doing?"

Charley Castle backed against the wall between the window and the bed. He said calmly, "Point that cannon somewhere else."

"What are you doing?" Molly asked again. She heard desperation in her own voice.

Clarence Hoffman advanced toward Charley Castle, aiming the revolver with one hand and reaching into his hip pocket with the other. "Lady, you don't take a prisoner without handcuffing him. Don't you know that?"

"Mr. Castle gave his word he wouldn't try to escape," Molly said. "He's kept his word, too."

Clarence Hoffman sneered. "That's the trouble with you women. A man tells you something, and you believe him. Women don't belong in this business."

Molly's rage choked off her reply.

Clarence Hoffman brought out a pair of handcuffs from his hip pocket. "Get on that bed, Castle. Go on."

Charley Castle did not move.

"Give me an excuse to shoot," Clarence Hoffman said with a laugh. "You'll be easier to handle that way."

"No!" Molly lunged and grabbed Clarence Hoffman's arm. "Don't! Don't shoot him!"

Clarence Hoffman was as strong as he looked. He flung Molly aside. She went sprawling to the floor. From there she watched Charley Castle get on the bed. Clarence Hoffman handcuffed him to the brass bedpost.

"Now, you ain't going anywhere," Clarence Hoffman said with satisfaction. "You're a man of your word, whether you like it or not."

Molly refused Clarence Hoffman's outstretched hand with a violent shake of her head. She got back to her feet by herself, ungracefully. Her hair had fallen out of place. She brushed it aside angrily.

"I'm sorry I had to do that, Miss Owens," Clarence Hoffman said.

"I am, too," Molly said in a low voice. She calmed herself and added, "You don't have to keep him in irons. Mr. Castle wants to go to Topeka to prove his innocence."

Clarence Hoffman smiled tolerantly as he shoved his big revolver back into his waistband. "Now, little lady, you just let me handle this from here on. Castle's a wanted criminal. That makes him more animal than man. He's staying in irons and I don't aim to let him out of my sight from here on. You had the luck of an angel getting him this far. We won't count on luck for the rest of the trip."

Frustration and rage caught up with Molly. She felt tears rushing to her eyes. Despising her own weakness and suddenly wishing she was a man, Molly whirled and left the room, slamming the door behind her. She went into 407, slamming that door, too.

Molly sat on the bed, fists clenched, refusing to cry, yet knowing she was. Clarence Hoffman was a mule of a man. She pictured him shoving and kicking the handcuffed Charley Castle all the way to Topeka. She would be powerless to stop him, short of shooting him. Clarence Hoffman was a dull man who took orders and followed them to the letter. Fenton operatives were told to handcuff their prisoners. That was all Clarence Hoffman needed to know. He was not a man who could imagine an exception.

The stupidity of the man and the situation boiled over. Molly slammed both fists into the mattress. With some satisfaction she saw two clouds of dust rise from the bedspread. So this hotel wasn't so fancy, after all.

Molly thought back over her instructions, trying to find some clause that would convince Clarence Hoffman it was unnecessary to handcuff this particular prisoner. But she knew it would have to be something in print, some specific passage in the instructions that she could point out to him. And she knew, too, there was no such passage.

Molly remembered something else. A footnote in her instructions had said her accumulated mail would be forwarded to the hotel. Molly got up. Looking in the mirror over the dresser, Molly assessed the damage, quickly composed herself, and left the room. She took the elevator down to the lobby.

The smiling clerk flipped through a stack of letters. He pulled out three for Miss Molly Owens. One was from an aunt in Pennsylvania, one was from Chick, and the third was addressed from the Circle 7 Ranch.

Molly walked out into the lobby and sat in an upholstered chair, glad to have something to take her mind off the infuriating problem at hand. She decided to open the letters in order of their importance. Chick's was first. The letter from the ranch, which aroused her curiosity, came next. Last was her aunt's letter. Molly already knew her aunt's cramped handwriting would only detail the current gossip going around about the relatives she had left in Pennsylvania.

After their parent's death in a train wreck, Molly and Chick had chosen to leave Pennsylvania to escape those very relatives. Most had been sympathetic to the point of cruelty, openly distrustful of one another, and intensely curious about the size of the estate. After the estate was settled, Molly and Chick left. Chick went west and ended up in Colorado. Molly went east to New York City.

Molly read Chick's letter twice, smiling at the postscript. And her brother was right about one thing: Two years was too long for them to be apart. She thought again of the irony of being within a hundred miles of Chick and not having the time to see him. In her present mood Molly would gladly leave Denver and catch the next train to Liberty.

Maybe it would be better all the way around if she did quit the case. Her employment with the Fenton Investigative Agency would likely come to an end if it was learned she had violated her instructions. And Clarence Hoffman was just the man to make sure it was learned.

Molly braced herself for the worst. Perhaps resigning now would be the best thing to do. She could write up a final report on the capture of Charley Castle, and resign.

But then she had another thought: What would happen if she left Charley Castle alone with Hoffman? Clarence Hoffman was capable of anything, including maiming his prisoner to make him easier to handle. He might warm up to the job by beating Castle. No, as much as she would like to, Molly realized she could not quit the case.

Stopped at this dilemma, Molly opened the letter from the Circle 7 Ranch. She read it and felt the hotel lobby, Denver, and the world slip away.

Dear Miss Molly Owens,

This is the hardest letter I ever had to write. Your brother Chick is dead. He was shot by Luke Standifer, marshal of Liberty. I can not even think straight enough right now to tell you the details. Will try to in a day or so. All I can say is that your brother was a fine young man, hard working, and loyal. He stuck by me through some hard times in the last couple years, and was doing so when he was killed. He came out here with a willingness to work and learn the ranching business. He done it, too. He will be missed around here and by all who knew him. I am so sad to have to tell you of his death, Miss Owens. Chick bragged on you often. I know he loved you.

Bess Tanner
Circle 7 Ranch

Chapter VII

The distant voices grew nearer. Men were repeatedly asking if she were all right. Molly opened her eyes and saw them peering down at her.

"My brother's dead; my brother's dead," she murmured.

A round-faced man held a glass of brandy to her mouth and tipped it up. The liquor went down hard and brought tears to her eyes. Molly sat up, coughed, and cleared her burning throat.

The round-faced man said with authority: "She's all right now."

But Molly knew she was not all right, and never would be. Two of the men helped her to her feet. The anxious desk clerk handed her letters to her; then in a barking voice he called for a bellboy to help the lady back to her room. Molly crossed the lobby and entered the elevator with a young bellboy tentatively holding her arm.

Alone in room 407, Molly stretched out on the bed, drained of tears, and drained of all emotions except sorrow. She felt weighted by a heavy and deep sadness as though she herself had experienced death. Molly knew she would never sleep again, never eat again, never laugh again.

Molly woke in the darkened room. She had no idea what the time was and didn't much care. She got up and went to the window and looked outside. There was no traffic on the moonlit streets below. She lit a lamp on the table beside the bed. Searching through her handbag, she found her watch. It was one-thirty in the morning.

Molly poured water in the basin on the dresser and washed her face. She felt weak and terribly hungry. She wondered how she could possibly get some food this time of night. Looking at herself in the mirror, seeing more age there than she liked, Molly brushed her hair and smoothed out the worst of the wrinkles in her dress. Doing that gave her an idea.

The elevator was not operating that time of night. Molly took the stairs down to the lobby. On night duty behind the desk a young clerk sat with his feet up, reading a *Police Gazette*. He jumped to his feet when he saw Molly.

"You're up late, ma'am," he said.

Molly smiled weakly. "Traveling exhausted me and I'm afraid I slept through supper. I wonder if someone could get me something to eat? Nothing fancy—cold meat and biscuits would be fine."

The clerk smiled too graciously. "I'm afraid not, ma'am. Everything in the kitchen is closed—"

Molly placed her hand on her abdomen and said softly, "In my condition, I really should have something to eat."

The young clerk's eyes opened wide. "You're . . . expecting?"

Molly nodded demurely. "I'm sorry to trouble you. . . ."

"It's no trouble, ma'am," he said quickly. "I can get you something. I often fix a bite for myself this time of night. How about ham and eggs? I can bring them to you. What room are you in?"

Molly put a silver dollar on the desk. "I'm in 407. Thank you so much."

Molly returned to her room. After climbing four flights of stairs, she felt dizzy and weaker than ever. She sat on the bed and tried to think back to the last full meal she'd had. She had not eaten on the train. Nor had she eaten in Silverthorne. There hadn't been time. When she had reached Silverthorne in the buggy and learned that Charley Castle was there and where exactly he was staying, she'd had no time to eat.

Her last full meal, Molly suddenly realized, had been in Colorado Springs! That was two days ago. And she remembered she had not slept since leaving Colorado Springs, either —not counting that fateful hour or so she had caught at the prairie train station when Charley Castle had freed himself. In her state it was little wonder that Bess Tanner's letter had brought her to a collapse.

Molly thought of that letter now, and of Chick. But when

she tried to picture him in her mind, his image slipped away like fog. He was there, yet he wasn't.

Molly answered the soft knock on her door. The young desk clerk darted in, carrying a tray covered with a checked cloth. With him came the smell of fresh cooked food and hot coffee. He set the tray down, glanced worriedly at Molly, and backed out of the room, mumbling that he wasn't supposed to leave his post and had to hurry back downstairs. Molly thanked him again and closed the door.

She sat on the bed and placed the tray on her lap. Molly ate steaming scrambled eggs and ham in gulps. For dessert she wolfed down three cold dinner rolls with jam. Sipping coffee from a porcelain cup, she felt stuffed and content.

Molly got up and walked around the room, from the window to the door and back again. Then she sat down and read the letter from her aunt in Pennsylvania. She sighed as she discovered she had been right about the contents of the letter: gossip.

Molly read Bess Tanner's letter again. Finishing it, she scanned Chick's. A thought had come to her and was nagging her now. Could there be a connection between Chick's death and the upcoming trial he had mentioned in his letter? Comparing dates on the two letters, she learned the timing was about right. Chick had never had the chance to testify in the trial.

Molly found herself pacing the carpeted floor. A floorboard near the window squeaked. Every time her pacing took her there, Molly stepped on that board as though punctuating her thoughts. And her thoughts, like her pacing, were running in circles. She had many questions and no answers. The answers were in Liberty.

The decision came with surprising ease: She would have to go to Liberty as soon as possible.

Having made the decision, Molly was left with the problem of Charley Castle. She could not leave him in the custody of Clarence Hoffman. And she could not spare the time to go all the way back to Topeka with the two men.

Molly arrived at her next big decision: Clarence Hoffman had to be eliminated.

An oversight now worked in Molly's favor. She had forgotten to leave the key to 406 with Hoffman. Molly had it in her handbag. The doors of the hotel rooms had no inside bolts; the only locks were in the latches.

Molly went into 406 as if she owned the place, holding a lamp in one hand, her derringer in the other.

By the light of her lamp, she first saw Charley Castle stretched out on the bed, wide awake.

"It's about time," he said aloud.

Molly shushed him. In the far corner of the room she saw Clarence Hoffman. He was slumped down in an overstuffed chair. On the dresser beside him was an empty pint bottle.

"He's out," Charley Castle said. "Get his key to these irons."

Molly tiptoed across the room, still afraid of waking him. She smelled him before she reached him. He reeked of whiskey. Molly set her lamp on the dresser, noticing the colorful label on the pint bottle showed an illustration of a charging lion. Clarence Hoffman was in no condition to charge anyone.

"Get his key," Charley Castle said impatiently.

Molly went through Clarence Hoffman's pockets and found the key to his handcuffs. She crossed the room and freed Charley Castle. Groaning, he got off the bed and stretched.

"Oh, do I have to go," he said, wincing.

Molly misunderstood him. "You aren't going anywhere until I say so."

"What I'm talking about doesn't have a thing to do with your say so," Charley Castle said.

"Oh," Molly said, turning away to conceal a smile. "Can you wait?"

"No," Charley Castle said. Then he asked, "For how long?"

"Long enough to get him tied up," Molly said.

"What for?" Charley Castle asked in surprise.

"We're leaving," Molly said. "We need some time to get ahead of him. He might wake up in a couple of hours."

"I doubt it," Charley Castle said.

"Let's not take any chances," Molly said. She added, "It's for your own good."

"That's what my mother used to tell me when she wanted me to do something I didn't want to do," he said. He paused, looking at Clarence Hoffman. "Look what civilization has come to. All right, give me your irons."

"Use his," Molly said.

"If I'm the one to tie him up, I aim to do it right," he said. "I need both pairs."

By the time Molly went into 407 and came back with her handcuffs, Charley Castle had gagged Hoffman with his own handkerchief and shackled his hands behind his back with his own irons.

Charley Castle used Molly's handcuffs in a curious way. He placed them between Hoffman's wrists, then drew one ankle back and up to the wrists and shackled it. He did the same with the other ankle. Clarence Hoffman was hog-tied.

"Help me now," Charley Castle said.

Together they lifted him on the bed. Hoffman groaned weakly, but never blinked. Charley Castle tightened the gag in his mouth, then straightened up and admired his work.

"Won't he be mad when he comes around?" Charley Castle said. "It'll take a blacksmith to get those irons off."

"It was thoughtful of you to put him on the bed," Molly said.

Charley Castle looked offended. "I didn't do it for his comfort. If he woke up on the floor, he'd bang around until somebody came in to find out what the trouble was. This way, he'll have to make up his mind to roll off the bed. That will take some hard thinking. He'll probably have to do it sooner or later. Maybe he'll break his neck."

"You have a devious mind, Mr. Castle," Molly said.

"It has served me well in the past," he said. "Now, let's go —so I can go."

They gathered up their bags. Charley Castle left a Do-Not-Disturb sign on the doorhandle of 406. They took the stairs down to the lobby and found the young clerk still reading his

Police Gazette. When he saw Charley Castle and Molly, he jumped to his feet.

Molly said over her shoulder, "It's later than I thought."

Staring, the clerk nodded and watched them walk out the front door of the Brown Palace Hotel.

"Later than what?" Charley Castle asked.

"It was a private joke," Molly said. "Lead the way to Union Station."

Charley Castle stopped at the first alley and ducked around the corner of a building. Molly waited patiently.

When he came back, he asked, "What took you so long to make up your mind?"

"About what?" Molly asked.

"About turning me loose," Charley Castle said. "I heard you pacing in your room for a long time. You had a squeaking board in there."

"I had some thinking to do," she said. "Sorry if I kept you awake."

"Not likely," he said. "You're a slow thinker."

"You don't know . . . anything," Molly said, hearing anger in her own voice.

Charley Castle said, "I know one thing: With Clarence Hoffman taking me back to Topeka, the odds of my getting there in one piece were slim. That's why you came and got me, isn't it?"

"That's part of it," Molly conceded.

"Well, what's the other part?"

"I don't want to talk about it," Molly said. "Let's go."

"The last time you hauled me away," Charley Castle said, "you had a buggy waiting." He looked in the general direction of Union Station. "This is going to be a long walk."

"We'll have the streets to ourselves," Molly said. "Lead the way."

Charley Castle picked up his carpetbag and samples case and started down the street, muttering, "Look what civilization has come to now."

After walking a few blocks, Charley Castle slowed up and

fell in beside Molly. He began talking to her. Molly realized he was trying to cheer her up. He told long tales of his past adventures in Denver, gesturing this way and that with his head, as though he believed he was giving Molly a good idea where certain events had taken place. Charley Castle's yarns were long and complicated, involving great numbers of people, including many local politicians. During all this telling and gesturing, he cast sidelong glances at Molly. She was aware of them, but was careful not to return them.

When they reached Union Station, Molly's arms ached from carrying her bags. They entered the cavernous waiting room. Overhead, the gaslights were turned low. Molly saw a few men sleeping on the long wood benches. Most looked like derelicts rather than waiting train travelers. Molly and Charley Castle found a polished bench that was unoccupied and sat down.

Charley Castle groaned and propped his feet up on his samples case. "Molly Owens?"

"Yes?"

"Thanks for getting me out of there," he said. "You just might have saved my life." He added, "I suppose this will get you in some trouble with your boss."

"It doesn't matter," Molly said. "I'll probably lose my job when Clarence Hoffman gets loose and files a report on me."

"He's nothing but a drunk," Charley Castle said. "Why don't you write up a report on him?"

Molly shook her head.

Charley Castle looked at her and asked, "What's eating on you?"

Molly did not reply.

"It might help to talk about it," he said.

"No, it won't," Molly said.

"I owe you," Charley Castle said. "I wish I could help you."

"There's only one thing you can do to help me," Molly said.

"Name it," Charley Castle said.

"Promise me you'll go to Topeka," Molly said. "By yourself."

Chapter VIII

Charley Castle was amazed. "Why would I want to do that?"

"Why, to clear your name," Molly said. "You want to do that, don't you?"

"Now, hold on," he said, raising a hand. "Let me see if I got this straight. You're asking me to turn myself in to some judge in Topeka?"

Molly nodded.

"Well, look what civilization has come to now," Charley Castle said. He asked, "Where are you taking off to?"

"I have some personal business up north," she said.

"So that's it," Charley Castle said, nodding. "Whatever's eating on you is up there."

Molly nodded.

"Well, it must be important," he said.

"It is," Molly said.

"Well, this sure puts me in a bind," Charley Castle said.

"I don't see how," Molly said. "You'll be able to prove your innocence and clear your name."

"Well, sure," Charley Castle said, too easily. "But I don't want to go out of my way to do it."

"What do you mean by that?" Molly asked.

"Well, look at it my way," Charley Castle said. "If those folks out in the Kansas flatlands want to accuse me of something, they can go right ahead and do it. A man like me has to learn to live with that kind of thing. Let them talk. I'm not going out of my way to stop them."

Molly said impatiently, "But you would if I took you there."

"That's a different matter altogether," he said. "You'd be taking me as your prisoner. That doesn't leave me a choice. But don't ask me to go out of my way to look for trouble."

Molly had to admit to herself that she saw the logic of his argument.

"If you won't go back to Topeka alone," she said, "I could turn you back over to Clarence Hoffman."

Charley Castle smiled. "Then you'd have that on your conscience, too."

Molly looked away from his sparkling eyes. Her bluff had not fazed him. She knew he was guessing. But he had guessed right. She held deep regrets about her brother. One was sharpened by his mention that they had not seen one another in over two years. Why hadn't she found time?

Molly realized she had been foolish to expect Charley Castle to turn himself in. She was only transferring her responsibility to him. No man would enter a lion's den when he had a way out.

Aloud, Molly said, "I don't know what to do now."

Charley Castle had settled in. His feet were propped up on his samples case, and his eyes were closed. "You got yourself a problem, all right," he said.

In a short while Molly heard him breathing deeply and rhythmically. She felt tired, too, but not sleepy. Her mind was alert as she thought ahead and tried to plan. The choices before her now were as clear as they had ever been. She knew if she took Charley Castle back to Topeka, she would get tied up with the case. Her experience in the past was that she would be asked to testify by either the prosecution or the defense.

Time worked against her. If a crime had been committed in the killing of her brother, the more time that passed, the harder a crime would be to prove. Witnesses' memories would become hazy. The killer himself might be long gone. Among lawyers Molly had heard a saying that she knew to be true: Justice delayed is justice denied. Counting the time it had taken for the letters to travel from Liberty to New York City and back to Denver, Molly feared too much time had passed already.

Molly's alternative was clear, too. If she left Denver and traveled to Liberty, she would lose her prisoner. Whether she would continue working for the Fenton Investigative Agency or not, Molly disliked the idea of not completing her assignment. And she felt that way even as she realized the job as a Fenton operative was nowhere near as important to her as learning the truth about her brother's death.

Molly was frustrated with her situation. She grew restless and got up and walked across the large waiting area to the main gate. The accordion-style gate was closed now. On a ledge beneath one of the ticket windows, Molly found a stack of train schedules. She read through them and learned the first northbound train was due to leave Denver at eight-fifteen in the morning.

Suddenly Molly knew she would not read further to find out when the next train to Topeka was due. She had made her choice.

Molly returned to the bench and sat down beside the sleeping Charley Castle. He was snoring softly now. Molly found Bess Tanner's letter in her handbag, along with Chick's letter and the one from her aunt in Pennsylvania. On the back of Bess Tanner's letter Molly penciled in some notes about what she would wire to the Fenton home office. She felt she must account for the action she planned to take, yet she was in no mood to set down her reasons in detail.

At last Molly decided to simply say there had been a death in the family and she had to leave Denver at once. The fewer details, the better. She decided not to mention Charley Castle at all, or that she had even met with Clarence Hoffman. The home office would learn of that soon enough, anyway.

Molly did not think she could sleep now, but after sitting on the hard bench a while, she swung her feet up on it and stretched out. She thought of all the uncomfortable benches she'd sat on in train stations since going to work for the Fenton Investigative Agency. There had been many. Molly could not remember one that was comfortable.

When Molly awoke, people were moving past her. In surprise she sat up, wondering where she was, and suddenly knowing. She saw travelers and well-wishers walking toward the ticket windows by the main gate. It was open now.

Molly sat up. She saw what had happened. Charley Castle was gone.

Well, I have lost my prisoner now, she thought. But it was inevitable. Her only plan for the morning was to once again ask Charley Castle to turn himself in. She knew he would never do it.

Molly leaned forward and at her feet saw a sheet of paper sticking out of her handbag. It was Bess Tanner's letter. Remembering she had not left it that way, Molly reached down and pulled it out. On the back, below her own scribbling, Molly found a note printed in large letters:

Molly Owens, you do not know this, but I had no intention of leaving Denver with you. I had to get out of Silverthorne, anyway, so I went along with you. Denver is as far as I go. What you do not know is that I stung the mayor of Topeka but good. He was one plucked chicken when I left that town last year, and it was not for any $800 like your warrant says. It was closer to $3,000. Served him right for trying to beat me at that pea game. Anyhow, you see why I can't go back to Topeka, with or without you. Up there in that room in the Brown Palace you stuck up for me and told Hoffman I was an honorable man. Well, thanks for saying it, but you gave me more credit than I was due. I am only honorable when it is handy. So long, Molly Owens.

C. Castle

Molly gathered up her things and found the telegraph office in the train station. She sent her telegram to the Fenton office in New York City. As she had planned last night, she said only that there had been a death in the family, she was urgently needed, and that she had to leave Denver immediately.

Molly bought a train ticket on the eight-fifteen northbound. She boarded one of the train's passenger coaches at eight o'clock. Finding an empty pair of seats, she put her handbag on the aisle seat, hoping to discourage anyone from sitting there. She sat next to the window, feeling in no mood for company.

The train, Molly realized, was almost twenty minutes late in getting away. She was suddenly time conscious and eager to be going. There was a last-minute rush of passengers, leading Molly to suspect they were the cause of the delay. The empty seats in the coach quickly filled.

One of the late-comers, a man wearing a battered Stetson and soiled work clothes, stopped in the aisle beside her. He put his bags in the rack overhead. In the nick of time Molly snatched her handbag from the seat as the man sat down. He had either chosen to ignore her hint, or it had been lost on him.

Molly glanced at him, then looked back out the window. He was middle-aged, with close-cropped hair and a fresh shave. In fact, as Molly stole a second glance at him, she realized his shave could not have been more than a few minutes old. A razor nick along the line of his jaw was bright with a tiny spot of blood.

The man brushed Molly roughly as he shifted in his seat. The train was just getting under way. Molly glared at the man, thinking she might make an appropriate remark about his behavior. His eyes met hers. Molly caught her breath and could not speak at all.

The man smiled and said, "Look what civilization has come to now."

Chapter IX

"Charley Castle!" Molly exclaimed.

He raised a hand, as though proclaiming modesty. "Thank you for the compliment, ma'am, but the name is Charley Tucker."

Molly stared at him. "What are you doing here?"

"Why, I thought I'd look into some mining properties up north," Charley Castle said. "I might do some investing."

Molly said, "Charley Castle, you're crazy."

"Charley Tucker is my handle," he said glancing at the other passengers. The noise of the moving train covered normal voices. Charley Castle added, "And don't you forget that, hear?"

With a clean shave and his hair clipped short, Charley Castle looked younger than he had before. Molly had thought of him as a man in his fifties. Suddenly he had shed ten years. He was a middle-aged man now, dressed in work clothes. But his hands were still smooth and delicate, Molly noticed.

Molly asked, "What are you really doing here?"

Charley Castle was slow in answering, as though he had several answers to that question and was trying to select one that was right for the occasion. "Well, for one thing, this was a fine time for me to leave Denver. Your friend Hoffman will have everybody in town looking for me. So I decided it was time for a change in outlook—and in looks." He paused and then added, "I got to thinking that I might as well catch a train."

"And it just happened to be this one," Molly said.

"I'd be stretching the truth if I said that," Charley Castle said. "The truth is, when I left you that little note, I happened to see a name in that woman's letter that caught my eye. It was the name of Luke Standifer. Well, once I saw that, I went ahead and read your mail—all of it."

Charley Castle fell silent. Molly guessed he was waiting for a rebuke. When none came, he went on:

"I did some deep thinking after I left you asleep in there in the train station. I sure am sorry about your brother. I can understand why it took the steam out of you the way it did. There is nothing sadder than the death of a young man. It's like a good promise that will never come true."

Hearing Charley Castle make such a remark surprised Molly, and moved her. Her eyes met his and held for a long moment. She looked away, feeling emotion well up in her.

"Anyhow," Charley Castle said, "I read your mail and got a fair idea of why you're going to Liberty."

"Do you know that man?" Molly asked.

"Luke Standifer?" Charley Castle said. "Sure, I know him by sight. And by reputation, too, like everybody else."

"What kind of reputation does he have?" Molly asked.

"Why, don't you know?" Charley Castle asked.

Molly shook her head.

"Well, look what civilization has come to now," Charley Castle said. "Here's a grown woman who carries a gun in her handbag, and she's never heard of Luke Standifer."

"Are you going to tell me about him, or not?" Molly asked.

Charley Castle said, "Luke Standifer is what they call a town tamer. That means he's a killer with a badge on his vest. I've seen the results of his work in many a mining camp in these Rocky Mountains, places where there wasn't any law but him and the big mine company that hired him. Sometimes a couple of mines would go together and bring him in. Standifer has started more than one boot hill in camps just like Silverthorne. Most mining camps don't need much law. Usually men can work things out for themselves. But with a man like Standifer around, they don't get the chance.

"The last I heard of him, he was working in Denver as a policeman. Then I heard he got fired because he didn't have any luck bringing in live prisoners. There was quite an uproar about him. Everybody in Denver was wondering what civilization had come to. Anyhow, he dropped out of sight after getting fired. There was talk he had gone to California. But, hell, you always hear that about somebody who hasn't been seen for a while. I always had a suspicion somebody had bushwhacked him. Plenty of folks would like to have done just that. So you can see why my curiosity was stirred up when I happened to see his name in that letter."

Molly nodded.

"You mean to tell me," Charley Castle asked again, "that you aimed to hunt up Standifer without even knowing who he was?"

"I'd have found out," Molly said.

"You sure would have," Charley Castle said. "And as soon as he found out who you were, he'd have shot you and claimed self-defense."

"Mr. Castle," Molly said with exaggerated patience, "I believe I can handle whatever comes along."

"You'd better start calling me Mister Tucker," he reminded her. "Or better yet, call me Charley. There won't be any mix-ups that way."

Reluctantly, Molly agreed to that. "You still haven't told me why you're going to Liberty—the real reason."

"Why, sure I have," Charley Castle said. "I'm going to look into some investments."

"No," Molly said, "I think you came along for another reason. I think you have some idea about helping me."

Charley Castle shrugged noncommittally.

"I don't want any help," Molly said.

"If that's the way you want it," Charley Castle said.

"It is," Molly said. "I don't want you to wander around Liberty, asking a lot of questions."

"I wouldn't do a thing like that," Charley Castle said.

"I mean it," Molly said.

Charley Castle said easily, "So do I."

"I don't see why you had to take a new name," Molly said, "unless you've committed another crime since I saw you last."

"There you go," Charley Castle said sadly, "accusing me of being a common criminal again."

"Who said anything about 'common?'" Molly asked. "A common criminal would have had sense enough to stay away from me."

"What do you mean by that?" he asked.

"You know what I mean."

"Do you aim to turn me in to the law?" he asked.

"That isn't my job," Molly said. "My job was to get you back to Topeka. I'll still do that if I get the chance."

Charley Castle smiled. "That's what I like about you, Molly Owens. You're steady."

"Where did you get those work clothes?" Molly asked.

"I bought them off a man," he said. "I paid him more than they cost him new because he had broken them in. I believe in paying a man for his time. And he looked good wearing that broadcloth suit of mine."

Molly asked again, "Why did you change your name?"

"I can't take a chance on Hoffman," Charley Castle said. "He might get serious about hunting for me. You never can tell what a drunk will do." He paused and said, "This Tucker handle is only temporary. I've done it before. As soon as things cool off, I'll go back to being my old self."

"Clarence Hoffman may never cool off," Molly said.

Charley Castle shrugged. "Maybe. Or maybe he'll get drunk all over again and forget about it. He may wake up a week from now, thinking the whole thing was a bad dream. But he's not your worry. You'll likely have your hands full with Standifer."

"We'll see," Molly said.

"You sure will," Charley Castle said.

"What else do you know about him?" Molly asked.

"Nothing good," Charley Castle said. He glanced at her and added, "Standifer has the reputation of being quite a ladies' man."

"I won't worry about that," Molly said lightly. "You have that reputation, too."

"What do you mean by that?" he asked.

"I mean, you can't believe everything you hear," Molly said.

"Look what civilization has come to now," Charley Castle said, as though offended.

The passenger train kept a northward course through the plains at the base of the Rocky Mountains. From her window Molly watched the scenery slide past at an even, relentless speed. Then at noon the train switched off the main line and followed a set of tracks that cut west into the mountains. The mountains here were similar to the snow-covered peaks around Silverthorne, though they were not quite as high or as rugged. Even so, Molly could not imagine cattle ranches in this region, and she wondered what lay ahead. By estimating the travel time, she knew Liberty could not be far away.

Early in the afternoon the train entered a narrow canyon. Steep granite walls closed in and sailed past on either side of the coach. The afternoon sunlight was blocked out, as though the train had entered a stone edifice. Then the walls fell away, the sunlight came back as suddenly as it had disappeared, and Molly saw what was ahead.

The narrow canyon opened out to low mountains and then to rolling hill country. The hills were covered with tall, green grasses and speckled with colorful flowers. Molly liked this country, as Chick had said she would, and when the conductor came through the car announcing "Lib-errr-teee" as the next stop, Molly felt a wave of excitement surge through her and she was glad she had come here.

The railroad tracks ended in Liberty. The train, after discharging its passengers and exchanging loaded freight cars for empty ones, would back through the canyon and the mountains to the main line.

Liberty's population was thought to be around five thousand. The town served the ranches and small farms in northwestern Colorado. Liberty had grown steadily and had become increasingly prosperous since the close of the Civil War when folks came to this part of the state with plans to stay. And recently Liberty had earned a reputation as a boom town.

The boom was due to the current rumor that the railroad had definite plans to run the tracks on west from Liberty, taking advantage of the natural passes through the mountains, and eventually on to California, making an alternate transcontinental route. Should the rumor become fact, Liberty would grow into a major center for trade and all manner of traffic and freight like Denver and Cheyenne were.

The immediate effect of the rumor was to make Liberty a speculator's town. Lots were marked off all around the original township. A dozen new houses and several business buildings and shops had been constructed in anticipation of a sudden increase in Liberty's population. They stood empty now, waiting for new owners and patrons. Vacant lots in town were offered for sale at enormously high prices. Choice corner lots were often sold two and three times—from one speculator to another. Each sale increased the asking price of these lots by half or more, and sometimes double the already inflated price.

Liberty's newspaper, *The Bell,* carried numerous editorials to the effect that this practice of unbridled land speculation could only create a financial bubble, and observed that one day all bubbles burst.

There was one fact no one in Liberty argued: The land speculators might be dreamers, but they were dreamers with money, either their own or investors', and their money had not hurt Liberty at all. The town was booming. And although the speculators were subject to steady ridicule from many long-time residents of Liberty, not even the loudest among them doubted that if the rumor became reality, all the landholders in town would be rich overnight, dreamers or not.

No one doubted, either, what would happen if the rumor turned out to be only a rumor: The expensive bubble would burst.

Molly Owens and Charley Castle got off the train and walked through the Liberty depot with the crowd of passengers and those who had come to greet them. The stone depot marked the end of Main Street. Charley Castle passed through the open double doors and stopped there.

Liberty's main street was lined with false-fronted buildings. Most were frame. A few, like the Community Church and the bank farther up the street, were built with granite blocks and red brick trim. On the other side of the street, past the Liberty Hotel, was the brick jail and marshal's office. It was noticeable from this distance because of its small, barred windows.

Molly stopped beside Charley Castle. By now she knew she should not be surprised by anything Charley Castle said or did, but she was surprised when he announced:

"Well, Molly Owens, we might just as well say good-by right here."

"Good-by?"

"Good-by," Charley Castle said, picking up his carpetbag and samples case. He walked into the street, veered out of the way of a loaded freight wagon, and stepped up on the boardwalk. Molly saw him enter the first saloon he came to.

Chapter X

Molly picked up her bag and trudged to the opposite side of Liberty's main street. Her feelings were mixed with disappointment and, despite herself, anger. She had told Charley Castle she did not need his help. But couldn't he have argued with her? A simple good-by was close to an insult.

Walking along the boardwalk, Molly glanced across the street at the saloon Charley Castle had gone into. It was called the Silver Dollar. Molly saw a huge silver dollar painted on the plate-glass window beside the saloon's batwing doors.

At the next intersection Molly picked her way through the wagon and horse traffic, walked through a choking cloud of dust, and stepped up on the boardwalk in front of the corner building. A sign over the door of this long, three-story structure read: LIBERTY HOTEL.

Molly entered the small lobby. An old man with more hair in his drooping mustache than on his head sat in a captain's chair beside the hotel desk. With an effort that brought a grimace to his lined face, he stood and greeted Molly. The chair he left appeared to be as old as the man. It was scarred, the arms were worn and stained from use, and the legs were held together with twisted wire.

"I'd like a room," Molly said, still tasting dust in her mouth.

"Fer how long?" the old man asked. The bottom fringe of his mustache was stained yellow from years of tobacco chewing.

"Forever," Molly said.

The old man laughed shrilly, ending with a cackle. "I don't aim to be nosey, ma'am. Sign here." He opened a green register and motioned to a pen. Beside it was a square ink bottle made of thick glass. Molly opened the brass lid of the bottle and dipped the pen into the black ink.

Molly wrote her first name, then stopped. She remembered something Charley Castle had told her.

"That there pen work?" the old man asked.

Molly nodded and quickly wrote, "Castle."

The old man turned the register around and squinted at the signature. "Molly Castle, eh? My name's Nate. Nate Stiles. The reason I asked how long you was staying was that I give over the best rooms to those who aim to be here a spell. The one-nighters and the drummers can get along in the rooms that ain't so good. Get my meaning?"

Molly smiled. "I'll be here a while, Mr. Stiles."

"Then I'll put you in a good room," he said. "Save you the trouble of complaining to the owner." He reached into a pigeonhole behind the desk and brought out a key. "I'll give you 17. That's a front one."

Nate Stiles came around the desk, grimacing with each step. He picked up Molly's bag with a gnarled hand. "Foller me, Miss Castle."

Nate Stiles gimped through the lobby and slowly mounted the stairs. Molly came along behind, thinking she was better able to carry the bag than he was. But she realized, too, that if she had offered, Nate Stiles would have been insulted. Who could understand men?

Room 17 was small. It was dominated by an iron bed with brass trim. Against the wall, by the tall, narrow window, were a chair and marble-topped dresser. Nate Stiles set Molly's bag on the floor. He was breathing hard now, through his mouth.

"Seventeen's one of the best rooms in the whole ho-tel," Nate Stiles said. "Gives you a danged good view of the street."

"I can see that," Molly said. "Thank you very much, Mr. Stiles."

"Aw, call me Nate," he said.

"All right," Molly said, extending her hand. "Call me Molly."

"Proud to," Nate Stiles said. He dragged his hand along his trouser leg before grasping hers. "It's a real pleasure to meet a gal who knows how to speak up for herself." He cackled.

Nate Stiles handed Molly the skeleton key to the room. He backed out into the hallway, saying, "Anything you need, Molly, water or anything, you just yell."

"Thank you, Nate," Molly said, closing the door.

Molly lifted her bag up on the bed and unpacked. She poured water from the flowery pitcher on the dresser into a metal basin, took a sponge bath, and then changed into riding clothes.

Looking out the window, Molly saw the wagon and horse traffic on the street below. She was surprised at the amount of it. Liberty was booming, all right, as Chick had said. Molly looked down at the far end of the block and saw a livery stable.

Molly descended the stairs and found Nate Stiles sitting in his captain's chair. Seeing him from this angle, Molly understood why he sat there. He had a panoramic view through the hotel window of one of Liberty's main intersections.

"Going out, Molly?" he asked.

"Yes," she answered, pausing by the desk. She had intended to ask for directions at the livery stable. But now she had another thought. "Have you lived in Liberty for a long time, Nate?"

"Nope," he said. "I don't like towns, never have. I only been in this here town for two years and four months. But I have chased cows in this country for most of my growed life. I worked as a cowboy until I got busted up. Then I cooked at the Bar M Bar up north of here. I never got the hang of cooking, though. I never much liked cooks. They're onery sons. So I done quit and came to town two years and fours months ago. Why you asking?"

Molly smiled. Nate Stiles was not an impolite man—just direct. "I want to ride out to the Circle 7 Ranch. Can you tell me how to get there?"

"Bess Tanner's place?" Nate Stiles asked. "Sure, I can tell you how to get there, easy. You a friend of hers?"

Molly nodded.

"I should have figured that out on my own," Nate Stiles said, cackling. "You're straight-talking, same as she is." He shook his head and added, "Bess has had a passel of trouble lately, though. Old man Dundee is plumb agin her. And to top it off, one of her riders got hisself killed here a couple weeks ago."

Molly held her voice steady and asked, "Did you see that killing, Nate?"

"Nope," he said. "It happened over on Second Street, right out in front of the Liberty Dance Hall. It was after midnight. The shots wokened me up."

Molly asked again, "How do I get to the Circle 7 Ranch from here, Nate?"

"Aw, that's easy," Nate Stiles said. "All you do is foller this street right out of town. Foller it west through the hills out yonder. Five, six miles out you'll see a big sign by a ranch road. The sign says JD Ranch. Well, don't take that road. Just keep on riding. Another half mile or so and you'll come to a ranch road that cuts off to the right toward Ute Mountain. That road used to be marked by a Circle 7 brand burned into a chunk of wood. I don't know if it's still there. Anyhow, it's the first road past the JD road. I know the JD is marked, big and proper. Justin Dundee is proud of that spread of his. Got a right to be, too, I reckon."

Molly left the hotel and walked to Benson's Livery. On the way she passed the red brick jail and marshal's office. A small group of men stood in the shade in front of the office. One, wearing a straight-brimmed Stetson, turned to look at Molly as she crossed the street. She glanced back at him and immediately wished she hadn't. The man wore a badge on his vest.

Molly hurried on to Benson's Livery and rented a saddle horse. She rode out of town on the westbound road.

Charley Castle had been inside dozens of saloons like the Silver Dollar. A long bar of polished wood ran along one side of the saloon. Behind it was a mirror with decorative flowers etched around the border. Over the mirror Charley Castle looked at a large painting of a nude woman. Smiling, she reclined on the floor of an idealized forest. Three white doves happened to be flying past, concealing the lady's private parts.

"Have another drink," the fat bartender said to Charley Castle, "and those birds will fly away."

"Believe I will," Charley Castle said.

He watched the bartender pour another shot of rye. After light conversation with him, he had introduced himself by presenting the bartender with an engraved business card that read: Charles Tucker, Geologist, Chicago, Illinois.

When the bartender had made tentative inquiries into his reasons for coming to Liberty, Charley Castle had answered evasively. The bartender quickly caught the hint, and moved on to his other customers at the bar. It wasn't polite—or good for business—to press a man.

Charley Castle turned now and leaned back on an elbow. Of the scattered tables out on the floor, he counted fifteen that were devoted to poker, faro, and twenty-one. From the Silver Dollar's proximity to the train depot, he judged this saloon would be the most popular one in town. But at this early hour, early afternoon, few of the gaming tables were occupied. Even the roulette wheel at the far end of the saloon was still now.

The Silver Dollar was a man's saloon. No squealing, money-grabbing saloon girls would be found here. As Charley Castle looked over the patrons, he saw many well-dressed men. They were crisp-talking, like city men. As Charley Castle kept hearing snatches of conversation about land values, lot prices, and the railroad, he realized these men were speculators. Apparently the Silver Dollar was their common meeting place.

A name spoken by the bartender caught Charley Castle's attention: "Mr. Dundee." Charley Castle stepped back from the bar to look at the man. He was white-haired, slender, and erect. He must have been a man close to seventy, but looked ten years younger. As Dundee glanced around the saloon, Charley Castle saw him scowl at the speculators.

Charley Castle turned back to the bar and drank a silent toast to the lady in the forest. He felt a mild regret that he could not work a profitable game in this town. With its speculators and atmosphere of wild rumors, Liberty was ripe.

Charley Castle was interested in a greater challenge, perhaps the greatest and most dangerous of his long career. In this game the goal was not money. It was a man. And within the hour that very man came through the batwing doors of the Silver Dollar Saloon. The fat bartender greeted him enthusiastically:

"Good afternoon, Marshal."

Chapter XI

Little over an hour out of town, Molly came to a large sign beside the road. It was suspended between two posts, and read: JD RANCH JUSTIN DUNDEE. The sign looked new, or freshly painted. Sharp black letters stood out against a white background.

Molly remembered Chick's mention of Justin Dundee in his letter. Apparently Dundee and Bess Tanner were engaged in a land dispute of some kind. Judging from what she read in the newspapers, quarrels over range land were common enough now. Range wars came in all sizes, particularly since the widespread use of barbed wire in recent years. Now, once and for all, ranchers were declaring what was theirs—down to the square inch.

The next ranch road that cut away from the main road was marked by a weathered board on a stake. Nate Stiles had a good memory. Molly could barely read the brand that was burned into the wood: Circle 7.

Molly followed the rutted, winding road back into the hills. Ute Mountain loomed ahead. The many shallow draws between the grassy hills were choked with willow thickets and cottonwood trees. Molly saw scattered bunches of cattle. Some were close enough for Molly to read their Circle 7 brands.

Molly topped the last hill and stopped. The breeze that hit her face was cool and smelled fresh. Below, the Circle 7 Ranch was cradled in the valley between this last hill and the rugged Ute Mountain that was dead ahead. The cottonwood trees gave way to pines and scattered clumps of aspens.

Among the trees Molly saw a corral, several patchwork outbuildings, and a log house with a chimney at one end. Smoke trailed out of the chimney and was swept away by the breeze.

As Molly rode down the hillside she saw a stream running through the valley, past the ranch buildings, and into a large meadow. There the stream meandered, reflecting the late afternoon sun like a gleaming snake. Molly reached the bottom of the hill and rode on to the log ranch house, feeling as if she had entered a colorful painting of a place that was too pretty to be real.

She reined up between a pair of tall pine trees at the log house's porch. Molly dismounted and tied the horse's reins to a tie post. Somewhere, behind the house and out of her sight, she heard the rhythmic sounds of someone chopping wood.

Molly walked around the house. Beside a shed she saw a woman splitting firewood. She was a stout, wide-hipped woman wearing a man's trousers and heavy shirt. The blade of the double-bitted ax flashed in the sun. Then as the woman came up with the ax, she saw Molly. Startled, she brought the ax down in a poor swing. The sharp blade glanced off the target, barely missing the woman's leg.

"I'm sorry," Molly said quickly. "I should have waited—"

The woman set the ax against the chopping block and smiled at Molly. "Oh, that's all right. I'm just clumsy. Have been all my life."

Molly stepped forward and extended her hand. "Are you Bess Tanner?"

"I sure am," she said, squinting at Molly. Then her eyes opened wide. "Oh! I know who you are! You're Miss Molly Owens!" She grasped Molly's hand.

Molly nodded as she shook the big woman's hand.

"Oh, how you resemble Chick!" Bess Tanner said. "I can see the resemblance in your face—and in your hair. His was as yellow as straw, too. Oh . . . oh . . . I reckon you know that better than anybody." Bess Tanner began to cry.

Molly put her hand on the woman's shoulder and comforted her.

"I thought I was all cried out," Bess Tanner said. She sniffed hard and wiped tears away with her sleeve. Clearing her throat, she said, "Come on inside, Molly. We'll have us a cup of coffee."

Bess took Molly by the arm and led her through the back door of the log house. In the kitchen Molly sat at a round oak dining table. She smelled food cooking. A Dutch oven was on the cast-iron cookstove.

Bess brought two porcelain cups to the table and filled them with steaming coffee. "I'm sorry about crying on you like that." She sat at the table across from Molly. "Like I said, I thought I was cried out until I seen you."

"We have reason to cry," Molly said.

"We sure do," Bess said. "There wasn't a finer young man around these parts than your brother. He was top notch. He's gone, and that's a loss that won't ever be made up." Bess took a loud sip of her coffee and added, "I reckon you've come to see his grave and to pick up his clothes and such."

Those were things that had not entered Molly's mind. She was amazed at herself. She had never even thought of Chick being buried somewhere. And of course he would have some personal items, along with a saddle and a horse. He might even have some money in a bank. Why had she not thought of these things before?

Bess went on, "You know, I had me an idea you might be coming here. I was going to write you a long letter. I had all the right words in my head, but I never got one wrote down."

"Bess," Molly said, "the truth is, I came here to find out exactly what did happen to Chick. The last time he wrote to me, he said he was due to testify in a trial of some kind in Liberty. I believe it concerned a dispute between you and your neighbor, Justin Dundee."

"That's right," Bess said.

Molly asked, "But Chick never had a chance to testify, did he?"

"No, he didn't," Bess said.

"What was the outcome of the trial?" Molly asked.

"Hung jury," Bess said. She added, "I don't know if we'll go to court again or not. I'm hoping Justin has had his fill of trials."

Molly said, "Tell me how Chick was killed."

"Well, as I wrote to you," Bess said, "he was killed by Luke Standifer, the town marshal in Liberty. I only know Standifer's side of the story. He claimed Chick tried to fight with him and went for his gun. Standifer said he shot him in self-defense."

"Do you believe him?" Molly asked.

Bess shook her head. "I don't believe it happened the way he tells it." She added gently, "From what I heard around town, I've come to believe Standifer killed your brother over a woman."

In the mirror beneath the reclining nude woman, Charley Castle watched the reflected image of Luke Standifer pass by. He stopped beside Justin Dundee. The two men moved to a table. They conferred intently for several minutes, then Dundee left, looking glum.

Standifer, however, smiled when he left the table and joined a loud-talking man near the end of the bar. Charley Castle had heard the bartender call him Melvin Goodwin. His full name, Mister Melvin Goodwin, had been spoken in a sarcastic way by several men at the bar. Goodwin was resentful, yet it was apparent he yearned for acceptance by the other men. He was a pudgy man who wore a derby hat cocked at a rakish angle. Goodwin spoke louder now than before as he basked in the attention given him by Luke Standifer.

Though Charley Castle had not seen Standifer for nearly three years, he would have recognized the man. He was tall and spare, yet he looked strong. In a cutaway holster tied low on his hip, Standifer carried a Peacemaker. And beneath the straight brim of his Stetson, Standifer's small, dark eyes darted around the saloon as Goodwin spoke heartily and somewhat drunkenly about land values.

Charley Castle finished his drink and turned to leave. When he was a pace away from the batwing doors, the bartender called out, "So long, Mr. Tucker. Come back and see us."

Charley Castle crossed the street and walked along the boardwalk to the Liberty Hotel. He had seen Molly head this way when he had first gone into the Silver Dollar. In the lobby of the hotel he was greeted by an old cowboy who introduced himself as Nate Stiles. He had seen Charley Castle come out of the Silver Dollar Saloon. He remarked that many men made a beeline for that place when they got off the train.

Charley Castle registered under the name of Charles Tucker. When he read the name above his, he realized someone else was using an assumed name, too: Molly Castle.

Nate Stiles was pleased when he was presented with the fancy business card of Charles Tucker, Geologist. He said he would give Mr. Tucker one of the best rooms in the hotel.

"The one-nighters and the drummers can get along in the rooms that ain't so good. Get my meaning?"

"That's an interesting policy," Charley Castle said. He glanced down at the register and saw that Molly was in Room 17. "How's 16?"

Nate Stiles considered the question, and nodded. "Sixteen's a good one. It gives you a danged good view of the street." He looked back at the pigeonholes. "I can give it over to you."

"That will be fine, Mr. Stiles," Charley Castle said.

"Aw, call me Nate," he said, handing him the key. "You need anything, Mr. Tucker, you just holler."

"Thank you, Nate," Charley Castle said, picking up his carpetbag and samples case.

Charley Castle went up the stairs and walked down the hallway to Room 16. He left his bags inside, then stepped back into the hallway. He went to the door of 17 and tapped on it.

When no one answered, Charley Castle brought out a ring of skeleton keys from his pocket. The eighth one he tried released the lock. He did not go in. He closed the door and locked it, noting the number of the key.

Charley Castle followed Nate Stiles's advice and ate supper

in Martha's Kitchen. Martha was a widow who served home-cooked meals in her own house. It was just around the block from the hotel. Nate Stiles said Martha was the best cook in the state of Colorado, and he wondered why some man had not come along and married up with her. Charley Castle wondered if that was a hint.

After a supper of steak and potatoes and dried apple pie, Charley Castle returned to the hotel lobby and struck up a conversation with Nate Stiles. After idle conversation, he asked:

"The town marshal here is a man with quite a reputation, isn't he?"

Nate Stiles scowled. "It ain't a good reputation to my mind. Standifer's nothing but a murderer. Everybody knows it, too —local folks, leastwise."

"It doesn't sound like he's very popular around here."

"Not with me, he ain't," Nate Stiles said. "Why, just a couple weeks ago he gunned down a young cowboy over on Second Street. Wasn't no call for it."

"Did you see it?" Charley Castle asked.

Nate Stiles shook his head. "I was here in bed. The shots woke me up."

"There was more than one shot?"

"Two," Nate Stiles said. "Standifer shot that young man twice."

"Didn't anybody see what happened?" Charley Castle asked.

"Nope," Nate Stiles said. He looked out the window and added, "Aw, that loco Cinnamon Sam claims he was a eye-witness. He'd say anything to make folks pay him mind. He figures Standifer is God's gift to the state of Colorado."

"Who is Cinnamon Sam?" Charley Castle asked.

"He ain't nobody," Nate Stiles said disgustedly. "He swamps out in the Silver Dollar and the dance hall over on Second Street. If you spend much time in the Silver Dollar, Mr. Tucker, you'll see him. He lives in a room over the saloon. The worthless little cuss chews cinnamon bark all the time. If he gets you cornered, he'll talk you to death."

Nate Stiles caught his breath and went on, "I reckon Cinnamon Sam thinks Standifer is an almighty great man because he has a lot of women and nobody kicks him around. Cinnamon Sam sniffs after him like a whupped hound, wishing he could trade places with him. That's how I got it figured, anyhow."

Charley Castle smiled at the old cowboy's observation. "Why was a man like Standifer ever hired as town marshal?"

"The goddamn town council voted to hire him," Nate Stiles said. "They got a-scared because Liberty is booming. They wanted a real hardcase to handle all the desperadoes that was supposed to land up here. Well, they got theirselves a real hardcase, all right. Now, ever'body's a-scared of *him*."

Nate Stiles spat into the cuspidor behind the hotel desk and said sarcastically, "Standifer's killed more men in self-defense than any man in history."

Charley Castle said, "In the Silver Dollar this afternoon, I saw Standifer talk to a speculator named Melvin Goodwin. I wonder if he's buying or selling land."

"Not that I know of," Nate Stiles said. "Why?"

Charley Castle shrugged casually. "I just wondered why he was talking to a speculator."

"Because speculators got money, I reckon," Nate Stiles said. "You don't have to talk to Standifer very long to find out he's inter-ested in two things: women and money. Right now he's pulling down the highest salary any Liberty marshal has ever had. And I hear he's asking for more." Nate Stiles paused. "Maybe he is doing some land speculation. Everybody else in this town is, seems like."

Nate Stiles studied Charley Castle. "Is that why you're here, Mr. Tucker? Are you buying up land?"

Charley Castle grinned. "I'll scout around some."

"Mr. Tucker, you're a little mysterious, ain't you?"

"I don't mean to be," Charley Castle said.

"You asked me a passel of questions," Nate Stiles said. "Mind if I ask you one now?"

"Not at all," Charley Castle said.

"Do you aim to open up a mine around these parts?"

Charley Castle laughed. "You get right to the heart of a

thing, don't you, Nate? I can tell you that a geologist always has an idea or two about mining. I don't have any definite plans, though."

"Now you sound like the railroad men," Nate Stiles said, laughing.

It was an hour past sundown when Charley Castle left the hotel lobby and walked back to the Silver Dollar Saloon. Nate Stiles had come to a conclusion that he hoped the bartender had reached. And he hoped the bartender would not keep the thought to himself.

Chapter XII

Molly stared at Bess Tanner and repeated, "A woman?"

Bess nodded grimly. "I feel terrible about telling you this."

"I want you to tell me," Molly said. "That's why I came here."

Bess gave Molly a long look. "You know, I remember Chick telling me you were an investigator of some kind. Do you have an idea about doing some investigating around here?"

"I intend to learn the truth about my brother's death," Molly said. "But I'm not representing my company now. Any investigating I do here is on my own."

Plainly, Bess considered this to be unusual. She said slowly, "Well, all I can tell you is what I heard in town."

"That's what I want to know," Molly said. "And I want to know what you believe to be the truth."

"That's hard to nail down," Bess said. "I knew Chick had been seeing a dance hall girl in town all spring. I didn't know how serious he was about her, but I didn't think he was lovesick."

Bess sipped her coffee and set the cup down, staring into it. "From the talk around town after the shooting, I found out that Luke Standifer had his eye on the same girl. He believes all the saloon and dance hall girls in town are his for the taking. Some folks claim Standifer and your brother had fighting words over this girl more than once."

"Were they fighting when Chick was killed?" Molly asked.

Bess shrugged. "Nobody saw what happened. At least, no witnesses have come forward."

"Tell me why you don't believe Standifer's story."

"Well," Bess said, "you probably know Standifer has an awful reputation. Some folks say he's killed more than twenty men. I don't know how true that is. All I know is that Chick wouldn't have picked a fight with Standifer. Chick wasn't a gunhand, and he knew it. Standifer knew it, too, I reckon."

Bess stared into her coffee cup as though she were looking back into a dark memory. "There was one thing that surprised me, though. The dance hall girl Chick had been seeing left town right after he was killed. Nobody's seen her since. I reckon she was mighty upset over it. Maybe she felt she was to blame. Anyway, she and Chick must have been thicker than I realized. My mind was on the trial at the time. Looking back now, I can see how things could have got pretty tight between the two men."

"What was the dance hall girl's name?" Molly asked.

"Jennifer," Bess said. "I never knew her last name. She worked at the Liberty Dance Hall."

Changing the subject, Molly asked, "What is this trouble between you and Justin Dundee?"

"Oh, that goes back a lot of years," Bess said. She looked at Molly. "Are you sure you want to hear all of this?"

"I'm sure," Molly said.

"Then we'd better have us some more coffee," Bess said, standing up. She refilled the two cups, then sat at the table again.

"My late father and Justin Dundee were two of the earliest settlers around here. Both were young men when they came here back in the '60s. In those days they were good friends. They had to be because they depended on each other. There was a lot of Indian trouble back then. But after my mother passed away, when I was a girl, my father changed a lot. He got it into his head that he should take over the JD. I guess you could say he got land hungry in his later years. He tried to buy out Justin, even offered him more than the JD was worth, but Justin wasn't any more interested in selling out than my father was. But my father never understood that. He went to his grave a bitter man because he couldn't shake Justin loose from his ranch.

"I never understood my father's thinking. If we had got hold of the JD, we'd have doubled our range land, more than doubled it, but we'd have doubled our problems, too. We'd have had to hire more riders, find a dependable foreman, and so on. As a family operation, we had all we could handle right here on the Circle 7."

Bess took a long drink from her coffee cup. "Well, to make the story short, not long after I buried my father, old Justin Dundee came riding into the yard—he hadn't even come to the funeral, mind you—and without even stepping down off his horse, he told me we was going to marry and combine our ranches." Bess shook her head as she thought back to the incident. "I don't know, maybe he thought he was doing me a favor. All I knew at the time was that no man could come in here like the king of England and tell me what to do. I knew I could handle this ranch, and I told Justin so. Besides, I didn't want to marry an old man.

"Maybe I wasn't very tactful with him, but I spoke my mind. Ever since that day, Justin Dundee has been trying to move me out of here, one way or another. This spring he accused me of pulling down his fences and butchering his stock. Then somebody laid a wet JD hide over the top pole of my corral out there. That same day Justin had me arrested. So we went to court."

Molly said, "But Chick had seen who pulled down the fences, didn't he?"

Bess nodded. "Last winter Chick went out after a storm to look after the stock, and he happened to see two JD riders yanking down their own fence. He came back and told me about it. We couldn't figure out why they would do such a thing. We guessed they were mad at Justin over something. If I had been on better terms with him, I would have reported it to him. But I didn't. After some JD stock wandered onto Circle 7 range, and then that JD hide turned up here, I saw what Justin was up to. He's getting plain foxy in his old age."

Molly asked the question that had been on her mind ever since she had left Denver: "Could Justin Dundee have hired Standifer to shoot Chick?"

Bess had been looking at the pattern of the grain of the oak table. Now her head snapped up. "Oh, no!" Then she smiled and said, "I can see how it might look that way to an outsider. As you can guess, I would have been acquitted if your brother had lived to testify."

"And Standifer wanted Chick out of the way, too," Molly said.

Bess shook her head. "No, Molly, it doesn't add up. Justin Dundee may be getting foxy and a little mean in his old age, but I can't believe he would have any part in a murder."

Molly did not argue. Bess probably knew what she was talking about. Yet the timing of Chick's death was too much of a coincidence. Perhaps Bess was too quick to give Dundee the benefit of the doubt. Molly wanted to talk to that man herself.

Molly asked, "How many men work for you on the Circle 7, Bess?"

"Just Barney Barnes now," she said. "I haven't hired anyone to replace your brother. I reckon I don't want to. Things won't ever be the same around here without him, and I guess I'm not ready to face that." She paused. "But I'll have to hire a man pretty soon. We're shorthanded. All the cattle should be up on summer range on Ute Mountain now. Barney has been driving them up there, a bunch at a time. He never complains, but he should have someone helping him besides me."

Bess pushed her chair back and stood. "Come on up the hill with me, Molly. I have something to show you."

Molly followed Bess up the slope behind the house. At the edge of an aspen grove ahead, Molly saw a picket-fence enclosure. Inside were four wooden grave markers. The one on the far end was new.

"This is where we laid Chick to rest," Bess said. "We got

the preacher from town to come out and give your brother a Christian burial. I hope it's all right by you."

Molly said that it was.

"My father is buried here," Bess said softly. "My mother is, too. Mother died in childbirth. The grave on the end here is my infant brother's."

"Chick wrote to me that he loved this ranch," Molly said. "He said that I would, too, and that I would like you. He was right, Bess."

Bess looked at her and smiled. "I'm glad to hear you say that, Molly."

When the two women walked back down the hillside toward the ranch house, Molly saw a wild man. He sat on the back porch, smoking a pipe. Hair covered most of his face. It was twisted and tangled and looked like it had not been cut for years—or washed. The top of the wild man's head was covered with green leaves.

"I should have warned you about Barney," Bess said in a low voice. "He's not like other folks."

Louder, Bess said, "Howdy, Barney. Ready for supper?"

"I am if you are," Barney said, standing up. He knocked out his pipe on the heel of his boot. He glanced at Molly, then looked at the ground between them.

"This here is Molly Owens," Bess said. "Chick's sister."

"I figured she was," Barney said, still looking at the ground. "I seen her earlier today."

"I hope you wasn't spying," Bess said.

"Nope," Barney said. "I just happened to see her."

"Well, come on inside," Bess said. "I'll dish up some vittles."

"No, ma'am," Barney said quickly. "You just hand 'em over to me. I'll eat out in the barn."

Bess winked at Molly. "All right, Barney. I've got the stew on the stove right now. Corn bread's in the warmer. I'll bring some out to you."

Bess took Molly by the arm and led her into the kitchen, closing the door behind them.

"Pretty ladies make Barney nervous," Bess said.

"I've never seen a man like him before," Molly said. "Why does he cover his head with leaves?"

Bess answered as she served up stew from the Dutch oven into a deep tin plate. "Barney claims a spirit up there on the mountain told him that if he kept green leaves on his head, he'd be protected from sunstroke."

Bess lifted three squares of corn bread out of a pan and put them on the edge of the tin plate. She poured a cup of coffee and started for the door. Molly opened the kitchen door for her.

"Here you are, Barney," Bess said. "You need more of anything, you just come on back."

Molly heard Barney answer, "Yes, ma'am."

Bess came back into the kitchen, smiling. "You're staying for supper, ain't you, Molly?"

"I'd love to," Molly said. "That stew smells delicious."

During the meal, Bess told Molly about Barney Barnes. "Barney's worked here ever since I can remember. He's getting up in years now. Barney's older than he looks because his hair has stayed dark." Bess laughed. "Maybe that's because it doesn't see water and soap often. At his age he shouldn't be going up to summer range alone any more—not that I could ever talk him out of going.

"I used to send Chick up Ute Mountain to Barney's summer camp with food and supplies to make sure Barney was getting along all right. Barney would stay up there when he knew Chick was down here looking out for me. Chick used to come back down here just shaking his head over the wild tales Barney had told him. Barney claims to see things. He doesn't know what they are and he can't describe them, but he sees them. Never mind that nobody else sees them—Barney does. He believes spirits live up there on the mountain. He probably got the idea from the Indians. In the old days the Utes laid out their dead in some caves up there.

"Barney says the spirits come out of those caves at certain times. They tell him all kinds of things about the weather and such. One told him about putting green leaves on his head. I remember one afternoon, after Chick had ridden down off the mountain and had heard a few tales from Barney, he said to me, 'Bess, I can't figure out if old Barney is a real prophet or a real madman.' And I says . . . ohhh . . ."

Bess Tanner's voice shook. She put her hand to her eyes. "Oh, Molly, I'm sorry."

"It's all right, Bess," Molly said, feeling her own throat grow tight. "I love to hear about him."

Bess looked at her. She reached across the table and touched Molly's hand. Neither woman spoke for a long moment. The feeling that passed between them was beyond words.

Molly helped Bess clean up the dishes that evening. Barney had left his plate and cup on the back step and disappeared. After Bess had washed the last of the dishes, she took off her long, stained apron and hung it on a nail beside the stove.

"Why don't you plan to stay around here for a few days, Molly? I'll show you what the Circle 7 looks like. There is some summer range up on Ute Mountain that you wouldn't believe. The Indians had it right when they thought the place looked like heaven." She laughed warmly. "And if you stayed here a while, you'd be giving Barney a chance to get used to you."

"I'd love to stay," Molly said, "but I can't. I have a room in the Liberty Hotel. I'd better be riding back there if I'm going to get to town before dark."

Bess looked out the kitchen window. "You won't make it before dark, Molly. Not by a long shot."

"I'll have to try," Molly said. "I really do have to go. I'll plan to come back for a visit soon."

"You do that," Bess said. "I'll get Chick's belongings gathered up for you. That's one more sad duty I've put off —like I put off writing to you and like I've put off hiring a man to take Chick's place."

Bess and Molly walked through the log house to the front porch. Molly tightened the cinch of the horse, and stepped up into the saddle.

Bess said, "I reckon I know why you're so anxious to get back to town."

Molly smiled down at the older woman. "I think you do, too."

"Well, you be mighty careful," Bess said sternly. "When that skunk Standifer finds out who you are, there could be trouble."

"He won't find out," Molly said, "until I want him to."

"How do you aim to swing that?" Bess asked.

"I'm going under another name," Molly said. "You and Barney are the only ones around here who know who I am. To everybody else, I'm Molly Castle." She saw no reason to mention that a man named Charley Castle knew her identity, too.

Bess laughed. "Well, ain't you the smart one."

"I'm counting on you two not to give me away," Molly said.

"Oh, don't worry," Bess said. "I won't let any cats out of the bag. Barney won't, either. I'll see to that."

"Thanks, Bess," Molly said as she reined the horse around. Over her shoulder she said good-by.

"Don't wait too long before coming back," Bess said.

Molly followed the ranch road out of the yard and up the hill. It was growing dark fast. Before she reached the main road, though, she saw that she was being followed. A man on a horse was behind her, keeping a distance of a hundred yards or so. Molly recognized him. He was Barney.

At the main road Molly let the horse have his head. The animal knew the way home and picked up the pace in his eagerness to get back to his stall in Benson's Livery. It was dark now. If Barney was still following, Molly could not see him.

Chapter XIII

Charley Castle pushed through the batwing doors of the Silver Dollar Saloon. Heads turned as men watched him walk down the length of the bar. Charley Castle knew immediately that the bartender had wasted no time in telling his customers the new man in town was a geologist from Chicago.

Spotting Melvin Goodwin near the end of the bar, Charley Castle purposely took the empty place next to the speculator.

The bartender said, "Good evening, Mr. Tucker. What's your pleasure?"

"Rye," Charley Castle said.

"Rye it is," the bartender said. In a surprisingly quick and graceful motion, he half-turned and reached to the back bar, grabbed a bottle of rye whiskey by its neck, uncorked it, and poured a shot.

Charley Castle laid a half dollar on the polished bar. "Double it."

"Yes, sir," the bartender said.

Melvin Goodwin chuckled and recited, "A rye-drinking man is a do-or-die man."

Ignoring Goodwin, the bartender asked, "Do you plan to be in town long, Mr. Tucker?"

Charley Castle took a swallow of the rye. "A few days," he answered.

"Will you be looking over some land?" the bartender asked.

Charley Castle nodded.

In an overly friendly voice, the bartender suggested, "Here in town, I suppose?"

Charley Castle shook his head. "Out of town."

"Oh?" the bartender said. "As a geologist, or as a land speculator? If you don't mind my asking."

"I don't mind your asking," Charley Castle said, "as long as you don't mind my not answering."

Several men at the bar laughed. Melvin Goodwin laughed louder and longer than the others.

The bartender cast a resentful look at Goodwin, then said, "Well, I reckon I earned that one." He nodded at Charley Castle and moved on to his other customers at the bar.

Melvin Goodwin nudged Charley Castle. He said loudly, "You interested in buying land, Mr. Tucker?"

Charley Castle looked at him. He was a pudgy man, and round-faced. The derby was cocked on his head at a rakish angle as it had been earlier in the day. Now Melvin Goodwin's voice was slurred, and he swayed slightly.

"My name is Melvin Goodwin, Mr. Tucker," he said.

Charley Castle nodded and shook his doughy hand.

"You are interested in buying land, aren't you, sir?" Melvin Goodwin asked.

"I might be," Charley Castle said.

"I have some choice acreage that I could sell you," Melvin Goodwin said, running the words together so that Charley Castle barely understood him.

Farther down the bar a well-dressed man leaned forward and said, "Mr. Melvin Goodwin has a lot of *choice* land he would like to sell."

Most of the other men at the bar laughed, including the bartender. Charley Castle realized that Melvin Goodwin was the butt of many of their jokes.

He said, "Burton, nobody's talking to you."

"Maybe that's why I don't get stuck with the kind of property you've bought," Burton said, laughing.

"I don't have as much money to throw around as you do," Melvin Goodwin said. "You're a rich man."

"I earned every penny of my money," Burton said. "I didn't inherit it. And I don't throw money around like some fools I know."

Melvin Goodwin slapped his small hand on the bar. "I won't take that kind of talk off you, Burton."

"Every man in here has taken plenty of loud talk off you," Burton said. He laughed in a taunting way.

Charley Castle could see that trouble had been brewing between the two men for a long time. It was rapidly coming to a head now.

Melvin Goodwin stepped back from the bar. He put his fists up in front of him. "Put them up, Burton."

Burton laughed.

The bartender said, "You're in no shape to be fighting, Mr. Goodwin."

Melvin Goodwin said to Burton, "Are you going to hug that bar like a coward, or step out here?"

Burton shrugged and said to the bartender, "The man leaves me no choice." He took off his broadcloth coat and stepped away from the bar, facing Melvin Goodwin.

The bartender swept up a sawed-off shotgun from beneath the bar. He said loudly, "I got nothing against a fair fight, but, gentlemen, let's keep it between these two men. The first man out there who throws anything—a chair, a mug, any-thing—is going to get his goddamn head blowed off." He waved the barrel of the shotgun from one end of the saloon to the other to be sure everyone understood. Then he spoke to the two men about to fight:

"All right, gentlemen. Have at it."

"This won't take long," Burton said.

Charley Castle got a good look at Burton now. He was nearly the same height as Melvin Goodwin, but he was slender and wiry. Burton went into a slight crouch and moved smoothly toward his adversary. Charley Castle realized this was not Burton's first barroom fight.

Melvin Goodwin got in the first punch. It was a straight right that landed on Burton's forehead. Melvin Goodwin's wrist buckled and he grimaced in pain. It was his last punch.

Burton came in fast, and low. He sank a hard left into Melvin Goodwin's stomach, then brought his right up in a swift uppercut. A dull, sickening sound of a fist striking flesh resounded through the still saloon along with a gasp from Melvin Goodwin's open mouth.

The uppercut straightened the pudgy man up. His eyes were glazed. Burton calmly set his feet apart and finished him off with a slashing hook to the jaw. Goodwin went sprawling to the floor.

Burton was hardly out of breath. He stood over the specu-lator and said, "You can't fight with your mouth, Mister Melvin Goodwin."

Goodwin groaned, but made no move to get up. Burton calmly put on his broadcloth coat, returned to the bar and leaned against it. The bartender surveyed the saloon. After making certain the fight was truly over, he lowered his shot-gun and set it beneath the bar.

Melvin Goodwin had no friends in the Silver Dollar Saloon. When at last he rolled over and got to his knees, no one came forward with an offer to help him to his feet. Charley Castle went to the man.

"Come on," he said as he took the pudgy man by the arm, "let's go get a cup of coffee." He led Goodwin outside.

They walked to a cafe a few doors away. It was growing late. The cafe was no longer serving meals, but Charley Castle managed to buy two cups of hot coffee.

Goodwin was bleeding from the corner of his mouth. He alternately blotted the cut with his handkerchief and sipped the thick coffee. He did not speak at all until he was nearly through with the coffee. Then he said in a low voice:

"Burton's right. I am a fool."

"We all have our moments," Charley Castle said.

Goodwin shook his head slowly. "I'm no fighter, even when I'm sober."

"That's a good thing for you to remember from now on," Charley Castle said.

"That's my trouble," Melvin Goodwin said sadly. "When I've been drinking, I think I can do anything. I always think I'm making big deals. But the next morning I realize I've bought the land that no one else wanted, at double the price." He blotted his mouth. "This afternoon I closed a deal on a quarter section of ranch land. It's cow pasture, and it always will be. I am a fool."

Charley Castle did not preach to him. It was likely that people had been telling Goodwin for years that he should stay away from the bottle.

"Do you own any land out west of town?" Charley Castle asked.

Melvin Goodwin nodded and said dully, "That quarter section is west of town a few miles. Hell, the railroad won't go that way. They'll have to angle north from here." He added disgustedly, "Hell, I knew that when I bought the land."

"Where is it exactly?"

"About five miles out," Goodwin said. "It used to be on the edge of the JD Ranch."

That surprised Charley Castle. "Justin Dundee sold it to you?"

Goodwin shook his head. "I bought it from Luke Standifer. We closed the deal this afternoon. I probably paid twice what he got it for. Hell, maybe three times the purchase price. Burton was right about me. I am a fool."

Charley Castle sensed that he was getting ready to apologize to the world. He quickly asked, "Did Standifer buy that quarter section from Justin Dundee?"

"I guess he did," Melvin Goodwin said. He held the handkerchief to his mouth and spoke around it. "I wish he hadn't. Then I wouldn't have made a fool out of myself today."

"Mr. Goodwin," Charley Castle said, "I'd like to take a look at that piece of land. Would you show it to me tomorrow morning?"

Melvin Goodwin perked up. "Sure, I would, Mr. Tucker. Are you interested in buying a cow pasture?"

"I might be," Charley Castle said. "I just might be."

Chapter XIV

Molly left the saddle horse at Benson's Livery and walked back to the Liberty Hotel. Though she was glad to have met Bess Tanner and to have seen the ranch where her brother worked, the experience had left her tired and drained of emotion.

Molly entered the hotel and went through the lobby without stopping to visit with Nate Stiles. Upstairs she unlocked the door to her room and stepped inside. A wall lamp hung on a bracket beside the door. Molly lit it, adjusted the wick, and turned around. Her heart leaped.

Charley Castle sat on her bed, leaning back on his elbows. "Good evening, Molly Castle."

Molly was startled, then angry. "What do you think you're doing? You don't have any right to sneak into my room."

"At least I didn't hide behind the door and poke a derringer into your ear," he said.

Molly felt her face grow warm. "How did you get in here?"

Charley Castle grinned. "How do you think?"

Molly realized they had been through this conversation before—in reverse. Charley Castle was obviously enjoying himself.

"All right," Molly conceded. "The shoe is on the other foot now."

"How does it feel?" Charley Castle asked.

"Tight," Molly said. She pulled the door shut. "I thought we said our good-bys."

Charley Castle sat up. He shrugged and replied, "I didn't mean it to be permanent."

Molly asked again, "How did you get into this room? You couldn't have used the same method I used in Silverthorne."

"That's true," Charley Castle said. "I have too much pride for that." From his trouser pocket he pulled out a large ring of skeleton keys.

"And you claim you're not a thief," Molly said.

"You won't find anything missing in here," Charley Castle said.

Molly shook her head ruefully. She crossed the room and sat in the straight-back chair beside the dresser.

Charley Castle said, "I saw you head for this hotel when I was in the Silver Dollar. And when I registered, I saw that you'd stolen my name."

Molly smiled. "As you once told me, that's the price of fame."

Charley Castle let the remark go. He said, "I was sitting here trying to figure out where you took off to this afternoon. Since Luke Standifer hasn't been arrested yet, I figure you must have spent the afternoon at the Circle 7 Ranch."

Molly nodded.

"What did you find out?" he asked.

Molly gave him a brief account of what Bess Tanner had told her.

Charley Castle said, "That's about the same story I got, too."

"I told you I didn't want you asking a lot of questions around town," Molly said irritably. "People will get suspicious. Then they won't talk to anybody."

Charley Castle raised his hand. "I'm not going to spoil things for you. The only man I talked to was Nate Stiles."

"I talked to him, too," Molly said. "He doesn't know much about my brother's death."

Charley Castle said, "Now, that just goes to show you that a man will tell another man things he would never mention to a pretty lady."

"What did he tell you?" Molly asked suspiciously. "He wasn't a witness to the shooting."

"But he knows someone who was," Charley Castle said.

Molly leaned forward in her chair. "Who?"

"A man called Cinnamon Sam," Charley Castle said. "He's a swamper for the Liberty Dance Hall and the Silver Dollar Saloon. Nate said he wasn't a very reliable man. But it seems to me he is better than no witness at all."

Molly nodded in agreement. "Where does he live?"

"In a room over the Silver Dollar," Charley Castle said. "I can find him tomorrow."

"Oh, no, you won't," Molly said. "That's my job. What does he look like? Which room does he live in?"

"I don't know," Charley Castle said with exaggerated patience. "I couldn't ask too many questions without making Nate suspicious."

Molly sat back in her chair.

"According to Nate," Charley Castle went on, "Cinnamon Sam shouldn't be hard to pick out of a crowd. He's a small man and he chews cinnamon bark all the time. Keep your nose to the wind. You'll find him." He asked, "How do you plan to question him without giving yourself away, Molly?"

"Leave that to me," Molly said confidently. She stood. "Why don't you go back to your room so I can get some rest."

Charley Castle went to the door. "I have a feeling you're cooking up some wild scheme. We'd better talk this over in the morning. You're likely to jump in with both feet and get in over your head."

"It's my head," Molly said.

"Look what civilization has come to now," he said as he left the room.

Molly lay on her bed. She wanted to rest until midnight. It was safe to assume that midnight was the closing time for the saloons. That would be a good time to locate Cinnamon Sam. She was eager to question him, but she realized she would have to be careful.

Half an hour past midnight, Molly left the hotel. She crossed the street and tiptoed along the boardwalk toward the train depot. When she was directly across the street from the Silver Dollar, she stopped. The saloon was the only building in the block burning lights this time of night. Molly had been right about the saloon's closing time. It was empty now.

She looked up the street. No one was around as far as she could see by starlight. In the next block she saw the soft glow of another light. That was where the jail and marshal's office were.

Then through the saloon window across the street Molly saw a hunched figure moving about inside. She was too far away to get a good look at the man. She walked on to the train depot. There she crossed the street and slowly made her way up the boardwalk. She stopped as she neared the lighted window of the Silver Dollar. As she edged up to the plate glass, she heard voices inside.

Molly listened intently, but was unable to make out what was being said. She advanced half a step and looked in. She saw two men. One was a fat man wearing a long white apron. He stood behind the bar, facing a little man on the other side.

The little man held a straw broom in one hand and used his free hand to gesture as he spoke to the fat man. As Molly watched, the little man stopped talking. He listened to the fat man, then reached into his trouser pocket. He brought out something that he put into his mouth. Though it could have been tobacco, Molly believed it was a piece of cinnamon bark.

Molly found the little man hard to look at, like a reptile. He was scrawny and unhealthy-looking, with a scraggly patch of hair on top of his head. His skull looked like a bullet that had been covered tightly with splotched flesh.

Molly heard the two men laugh at something one had said; then she heard the loud scuff of a boot heel on the boardwalk.

Molly whirled and saw a man emerge from the shadows in front of the hardware store next door. Molly's mouth went dry as the man stepped into the patch of light that streamed through the window of the Silver Dollar Saloon.

"You looking for somebody, ma'am?"

Molly shook her head. She could not speak. The man's face was kept in shadow by the straight brim of his Stetson. Molly's eye was caught and held almost hypnotically by a metal star on the man's vest. The badge gleamed with reflected light.

The marshal started to speak again, but Molly lunged around him and ran. Her shoes thumped loudly on the planks of the boardwalk. At the corner building she turned and stopped, desperately hoping Standifer was not following.

After hearing nothing but her own pulse drumming in her head, Molly peeked around the building in time to see the marshal standing in front of the saloon door. Molly's breath rasped through her throat and tasted like blood. She had never been so frightened. Luke Standifer had come from nowhere, like a ghost.

He must have knocked on the door. For as Molly watched, the door opened and the marshal was bathed in yellow light. He stepped inside. The door closed behind him.

Molly picked up her skirt and ran across the intersection to the hotel. When she entered the lobby, her breathing was still ragged, but her fear had subsided.

She tiptoed up the stairs. In her room she undressed without lighting a lamp and climbed into bed, feeling glad to be there.

When Molly woke, sunshine streamed in through the window like bright, fluid gold. The gold laid upon the floor, measured into long rectangles by the window panes. The nightmare was still fresh in her mind even as she sat up in bed and stretched. A faceless man had leaped out of a deep shadow. He spoke in a rough voice, promising to kill her. Then he melted back into the shadow, only to emerge when Molly tried to run. The faceless man repeated his evil threat and faded back into the shadow once again. The more Molly tried to get away, the stronger the threats became, and she knew escape from this powerful man was impossible.

Molly ate a late breakfast. She followed Nate Stiles's advice and walked around the block from the hotel to a house in a block of residences that had a small sign over the door: MARTHA'S KITCHEN. Mounting the few steps to the porch, Molly opened the door and entered Martha's house. The front room and living room were crowded with tables and chairs. All the tables were covered with blue checked cloths and neatly arranged place settings.

The breakfast crowd was gone. Molly sat at a small table near the kitchen and ordered breakfast from Martha herself. Martha was a large, smiling woman who kept her hair tied in a long braid that ran down her back. The breakfast was a good one: scrambled eggs laced with ham, hot bread and orange marmalade, and fresh-ground coffee.

When she finished eating, Molly was joined by Martha. The two women drank coffee together and got acquainted. Molly answered her few personal questions vaguely. Martha invited her to church and was chatting about her life since her husband died when she looked out the front window and suddenly stopped talking. The big woman got up and rushed into the kitchen.

Molly saw the front door swing open. A tall man entered. He looked around, then came lumbering toward Molly. He put a hand to his Stetson.

"Miss Molly Castle?" he asked.

Molly nodded, unable for a moment to take her eyes from

the badge on his vest. In that instant she was thrown back into her dream of the faceless man.

"I'm Luke Standifer," he said, "town marshal here."

Molly nodded again.

"I'm sorry if I scared you last night," he said. "I didn't aim to."

Molly was still unable to think of a sensible reply.

Standifer said, "I hope you believe me, ma'am."

Molly managed a smile.

Standifer took this as an invitation and sat down at the table. "I found out who you was by checking all the hotels. It wasn't hard to track you down. Most folks go to the Liberty, even though old man Stiles is an onery cuss. He's tight-mouthed, too. But I finally got it out of him who you was. I wanted to find you first thing this morning so I could tell you I'm sorry about scaring you."

"I . . . I accept your apology, Marshal," Molly said.

Standifer grinned. "Was you looking for somebody last night, or what?"

Molly's thoughts raced ahead. She realized an opportunity was here and her mind searched for a way to turn it to her advantage.

"Yes," she said tentatively.

"Well, who?" Standifer asked.

Molly's thoughts froze. She could not think of a single name. "It's a personal matter, Marshal."

"Well, I figured that," he said. "Don't you worry. I'm not one to gab around town about things. Anything you tell me won't get no farther than right here."

When Molly failed to reply, Standifer went on, "I just might be able to help you out. I get flyers and wanted posters in my office every week."

He let that sink in, then said, "I can tell you for sure there ain't much going on in this town that I don't know about, Miss Castle. I got this town in my pocket."

His lack of modesty brought a smile to Molly's face. Standifer misunderstood it and smiled back. "Now, just who are you hunting?"

Molly realized she had to come up with something. If she did not, this opportunity would be lost. The first name that came to her mind was Abraham Lincoln. The second was Charley Castle.

"Charley Castle?" Standifer said in surprise. "You mean Charley Castle, the confidence man? He's a famous man. You a relation of his?"

Molly nodded shyly.

Standifer asked, "What's he to you?"

"Charley Castle is my . . . husband," Molly said experimentally.

"Husband?" Standifer asked, looking at her left hand. "I thought you was single."

"I am . . . now," Molly said, wondering how all this must sound.

"What did he do, run off from you?" Standifer asked.

"Yes," Molly said.

"A man would be pure loco to run off from a fine-looking woman like you," Standifer said.

Molly lowered her eyes.

"Now that I think on it," Standifer said, "I've heard tell some things about Charley Castle. I've never met the man, but I have seen him a couple of times. He has a full beard and he dresses fancy. He's gambler and a showman. They say he's quite a man with the ladies."

"I found that out," Molly said, "too late."

"When I saw you last night," Standifer said, "I kind of thought you was hunting for somebody like your husband or your daddy. I was going to chase after you, but I figured I'd only scare you more. Did you see Castle go into that saloon?"

"No," Molly said. "I don't even know if he's in Liberty or not. I came here to visit my friend Bess Tanner. While I'm here I thought I might happen to see my former husband. But I couldn't very well be around a saloon when folks might see me."

Standifer nodded seriously. "What you need is a man to

help you—especially a man like me. If that no-good Charley Castle comes to Liberty, I'll know about it."

Molly nodded appreciatively.

"What makes you think he might be here?" Standifer asked.

Molly looked away. She could not think of an answer.

Standifer said, "The last I heard of Charley Castle, he was down in Denver. Did you hunt around down there?"

Molly said, "He was thrown out of Denver."

"He was, huh?" Standifer said, smiling. He apparently took pleasure in that thought.

"A man in Denver told me he was headed north," Molly said.

"Well, maybe he went to Cheyenne," Standifer said.

"I'll go there next," Molly said.

Standifer nodded thoughtfully. "Why are you hunting for him, anyway? If he was crazy enough to run off from a woman like you, why don't you let him go?"

Molly had not foreseen that question. Like a tightrope walker who was losing balance, she said, "He ran off with my family's life savings."

Standifer slapped his thigh. "That no-good son . . ." His voice trailed off in deference to the lady. "If he shows up in my town, there will be hell to pay. He's done wrong and he'll pay for it."

Molly swallowed hard. "I wouldn't want him hurt, Marshal."

"From now on, you leave things to me," Standifer said. "I'll look into this right directly. I'll talk to gamblers and saloon keepers. I'll find out where he is." Standifer glanced back toward the kitchen door. "I can't even get a cup of coffee in here. I don't know how that fat woman stays in business, onery as she is." He stood. "Well, I'll be on my way. You'll be hearing from me."

Standifer stomped out of the dining room, casting an angry look into the kitchen as he passed by. He went out, leaving the front door standing open behind him.

Martha stormed out of the kitchen like a warship. She closed the door and came to Molly's table.

"God forgive me, but I despise that man. He's a murderer who has done his evil work from one end of this state to the other. It'll be a long day in winter before he'll get a thing to eat or drink in my house."

She studied Molly for a moment, then said, "I'll speak plain to you, Miz Castle, since you're new in town. Standifer grabs up every woman he can get hold of. Usually he takes to saloon girls. I can see he's taken a shine to you. I hope you don't let him bother you."

Molly had an idea of bothering Standifer. She wished she could say that to Martha. Instead she said:

"Don't worry, Martha. I won't."

Molly left Martha's Kitchen and walked back to the Liberty Hotel. She tried to see where this new turn of events would lead her. Being on speaking terms with Standifer so soon was more than she had hoped for. But she felt guilty for saying those awful things about Charley Castle. She would have to warn him as soon as possible that Standifer was looking for a bearded confidence man named Charley Castle.

Chapter XV

Along with a swollen jaw and a sore right hand, Melvin Goodwin had a violent headache in the morning. As agreed the previous night, Charley Castle joined the speculator for breakfast in the cafe near the Silver Dollar Saloon.

Goodwin greeted him with an embarrassed, "I shouldn't drink," complained of his headache, and then the two men ate breakfast in silence. Afterward they rented a buggy at Benson's Livery.

Melvin Goodwin, favoring his right hand, drove the buggy out of town on the westbound road. The road wound through a forest of lodgepole pines, often broken by grassy pasture-land. Goodwin turned off on the road marked by the JD sign. Nearly two miles back in the rolling hills, a ranch house came into view. The house was one story, not small, but it was almost dwarfed by a huge white barn.

"There's the JD headquarters," Melvin Goodwin said.

"Quite a place," Charley Castle said. "What kind of man is Justin Dundee?"

"I don't know him well," Goodwin said. "He's a strong-minded old boy. Set in his ways, according to Luke Standifer."

"Are they good friends?" Charley Castle asked.

Goodwin shrugged. "Standifer doesn't strike me as a man who has close friends." He added, "I guess the same could be said of me."

Melvin Goodwin turned the buggy off the ranch road before reaching the ranch house. He followed the faint track of wagon ruts through a grassy meadow for half a mile, then drove the team up a hillside. At the top he pulled the horses to a halt. Below was another wide, grassy meadow. A small stream, marked by a thick growth of willows, ran through the meadow.

Goodwin said, "The quarter section I bought from Standifer includes most of this meadow, Mr. Tucker. It isn't fenced off from the JD. I think Standifer had an agreement with Dundee to leave this range open. If you were to buy the land, I'd fence it for you. I have no binding agreement with Dundee. I own this land, free and clear."

"What about that far hillside?" Charley Castle asked.

"I'm afraid I own that, too," Goodwin said. "It's rocky as all hell."

Charley Castle climbed out of the buggy. He looked across the meadow. At the base of the hillside there was a large out-cropping of granite. It was a solid piece of rock, about twice the size of a house. Or the size of Dundee's white barn, Charley Castle mused.

Goodwin continued, "Like I told you last night, Mr. Tucker, I've made some bad deals in my lifetime, but this one is probably the worst. There is no way in hell the railroad will ever come this way. Everybody knows the rail line will have to cut around Ute Mountain, then go due west. All that land has already been bought up." He added, "I'd be lying if I told you the railroad might lay steel through here one day."

Charley Castle looked at the pudgy speculator. "I appreciate your honesty, Mr. Goodwin."

"You helped me out last night," he said. "I'm not one to forget that."

Charley Castle looked back the way they had come. The ranch headquarters was out of sight from here. And because of the hill, it would be out of sight from the big rock outcropping, too. Out of sight, but not out of earshot, Charley Castle thought. He climbed back up into the buggy.

"Would you be interested in leasing this property?"

"Lease?" Goodwin asked in surprise. "You want to lease this whole quarter section?"

Charley Castle nodded. "If my offer is right for you."

"What do you have in mind?" Goodwin asked.

"Sixty days," Charley Castle said, "at one thousand dollars, paid in advance."

Melvin Goodwin blinked. "That's a lot of money, Mr. Tucker. Are you sure you know what you're doing?"

Charley Castle smiled. "I believe so."

"Well, you've made yourself a deal," Goodwin said. "Yes, sir, I couldn't turn you down on a deal like that. What do you plan to do with this land?"

"That doesn't have to be in our lease agreement, does it?" Charley Castle asked.

"Why, no," Goodwin said slowly.

"You won't place any restrictions on my use of the land, will you?" he asked.

"Not at five hundred dollars a month," Goodwin said, laughing. "This is the first profit I've made since I came to Liberty."

"Let's get back to town and draw up a document," Charley Castle said. He looked at his pocket watch. "We'll have to hurry some. I have a train to catch this afternoon."

Goodwin turned the buggy and started down the hillside.

He glanced at the man he knew as Charles Tucker. "I've never in my life met a man like you before, Mr. Tucker."

That afternoon Molly heard the final blast of the train whistle before it left the depot for its daily run back to Denver. For the third time that day, she tapped on the door of Charley Castle's room. Still there was no answer.

Molly wondered where he could be. She felt more and more guilty about the yarn she had told Standifer, and she wanted to relieve her guilt by warning Charley Castle.

Resigned to the fact that Charley Castle was either out of town or in the back corner of a smoke-filled saloon pretending he was new to the game of poker, Molly left the hotel. She took a walk around town that was intended to appear leisurely.

She followed the boardwalk to the train depot. Liberty's idlers, having seen the train off, were wandering back to the saloons. At the depot Molly crossed Main. Instead of walking up the other side, she strolled down First Street. This graded street led to the residential section. Molly turned at the first block and walked up the avenue that paralleled Main. Here she saw tidy frame houses. The fancier ones boasted bay windows and ginger-bread decorations and wrought-iron fences.

Molly looked past these houses and studied the rear of the stores on Main Street. She was able to pick out the Silver Dollar Saloon. A covered staircase angled up the back. On the second story were half a dozen windows. Cinnamon Sam must live behind one of them, she thought.

Turning on Second Street, Molly walked back toward Main. Benson's Livery was ahead. Then, to her left, she saw the Liberty Dance Hall. It looked much like a barn, but was gaudily painted. In front she saw an even row of posts, as high as a man. Lanterns were mounted on top. At night the place might look festive. By day it looked sad, like a Christmas tree on the day after Christmas.

But perhaps the Liberty Dance Hall looked sad only to Molly. In front of this brightly painted building was the site of her brother's death. She barely glanced at the ground here, then hurried on to Main Street.

In the lobby of the hotel she was greeted by Nate Stiles. Molly stopped at the desk. To make conversation, she asked how he was feeling.

"Aw, I feel fit enough," he said. He added, "As good as I can expect since I got busted up."

"How did you get hurt?" Molly asked.

Nate Stiles looked out the window. After a long moment he said, "Throwed."

Molly sensed, too late, that it was something he did not want to talk about. She regretted asking.

Still looking out the window, the old cowboy said in a low voice, "Horse landed on me."

"I'm sorry," Molly said, feeling uncomfortable and embarrassed. She had touched a point that should not have been disturbed: the end of a man's working life.

At suppertime Molly left the hotel and walked to Martha's Kitchen. On the way she was stopped by Luke Standifer.

"Good evening, Mrs. Castle," he said, touching his Stetson.

Molly found that she could only glance at him. She nodded in reply.

"Like I promised you, I've been asking around about your former husband," Standifer said. "Don't worry, I ain't told nobody he is your former husband. I just ask questions. I don't have to tell why I'm asking. A gambler told me Castle wintered in Colorado Springs. He said Castle was courting a widow down there."

Molly felt a wave of fear as she realized Standifer was probing the truth of her story. Could he have found a hole in it?

Molly said, "I don't know who he was courting last winter, Marshal."

"You wasn't married to him then?" Standifer asked.

Molly shook her head.

Standifer apparently took comfort in this development. "That's what I figured. You wasn't married very long, was you?"

Molly shook her head again. "But I don't see what that has to do with your investigation here."

Standifer's smile faded at this small reprimand. "Nothing, I reckon," he said; then he blurted, "I want you to have supper with me tonight."

"No, Marshal, I can't." Molly turned and walked on toward Martha's Kitchen.

"Some other time," Standifer called after her. "I have to talk to you about some things."

Molly kept walking, making no sign that she had heard.

After supper that evening, she lay on her bed. She had hoped to rest until midnight. But every time she drifted toward sleep, her dream of the faceless man returned, and she would jerk awake in fear.

At midnight she got out of bed, feeling tired and groggy. She wished for a cup of coffee, knowing the wish would go unanswered. She went downstairs and left the hotel.

Outside there was no moon. Molly stood in front of the hotel and breathed deeply of the cool night air. Her head cleared as she thought to the job ahead. Farther down the street, lamplight spilled out of the window of the Silver Dollar Saloon.

Molly tiptoed along the boardwalk, stopping when she was directly across the street from the saloon. She moved back into the recessed doorway of a millinery shop.

In the saloon she saw two men moving about. This time she recognized them: the fat, white-aproned bartender and the small, hunched figure of Cinnamon Sam.

Molly judged she had stood in the doorway half an hour when she saw a man walking down the street. He came slowly and deliberately. Though she had only starlight to see the man by, Molly knew he was Luke Standifer. And then she realized he was surveying the store fronts. Molly pressed herself against the door of the millinery shop, feeling her pulse quicken. Standifer drew nearer and appeared to look right at her.

But then he moved into the patch of light cast by the saloon, looked on past the doorway that concealed Molly, and turned.

He stepped up on the boardwalk and tapped on the saloon door.

Molly heard his footfalls on the planks of the boardwalk. She realized then that he must walk in the street to soften the sounds of his footsteps. That explained how he was able to sneak up on her last night.

Tonight will be different, she thought; now she knew where *he* was.

The fat bartender opened the door. He let the marshal in and closed the door behind him. Molly hurried across the street. She tiptoed over the boardwalk, then entered the narrow passageway between the Silver Dollar and the hardware store next door. In the back alley she turned the corner behind the store. That afternoon she had spotted this as a good place to wait for Cinnamon Sam.

The wait was a long one. There was not enough light in the back alley for her to read her watch, but she guessed the time to be close to one in the morning when she heard the door of the saloon open. She heard mumbled good-bys, then the door closed, and there was silence. From the voices Molly realized Standifer had left.

After another half an hour, Molly judged, the front door of the saloon opened again. Molly heard both the voices of the bartender and Cinnamon Sam. For a frightening moment Molly wondered if the bartender lived in a room over the saloon, too, and would be with Cinnamon Sam when he came to the back stairs. But then she heard them say good-by and heard the bartender's heavy footfalls on the boardwalk. Cinnamon Sam came walking down the passageway between the two buildings, mumbling to himself.

The stooped figure of Cinnamon Sam came into Molly's view when he reached the back alley. He turned and took a step toward the staircase. Molly leaped out at the little man from behind, jamming her derringer into the back of his neck.

Cinnamon Sam threw his hands into the air and cried out, "Don't shoot me! Don't shoot me!"

"Quiet!" Molly said. "Be quiet."

Surprised at hearing a woman's voice, Cinnamon Sam

quieted and started to turn around. "Wha—what do you want?"

"Don't move," Molly said in a low voice. "I don't want to shoot, but I will if I have to."

"I ain't got no money," Cinnamon Sam said, turning again.

Molly smelled cinnamon. She jammed the derringer harder into his neck. "Don't turn around!"

"I ain't got no money," he said again.

"I don't want money," Molly said. "I want information."

"I don't know nothing," Cinnamon Sam said.

"Yes, you do," Molly said. "And the only way you're going to get out of here alive is to answer my questions."

"What questions?" Cinnamon Sam's voice rose in fear.

"You saw Standifer shoot that cowboy from the Circle 7, didn't you?"

Cinnamon Sam started to answer, then stopped.

Molly prodded him with her derringer.

"Sure, I seen it."

"What did you see?"

Cinnamon Sam said, "Luke shot that cowboy in self-defense."

"No," Molly said, prodding him again. "What did you *see?*"

"They was arguing," Cinnamon Sam said. "I was swamping out the dance hall, and I heard them arguing out in front. I thought ever'body had went home, so I went outside and looked. The lamps was still lit up. I seen them plain as day. I didn't know what they was arguing over until I seen Jennifer."

"She was there?" Molly asked.

"Sure, she was," Cinnamon Sam said. "Jennifer was the purtiest girl in Liberty. Luke and that cowboy was arguing over her. Afterwards, she started screaming."

"What happened?" Molly asked.

"Luke shot him in self-defense."

Molly thumbed back the hammer of the derringer.

"No!" Cinnamon Sam cried.

"You have three seconds to tell me what you saw," Molly said. "One, two—"

"Wait!" Cinnamon Sam said. "I'll tell you. Luke, he knocked that cowboy to the ground. That cowboy never should have argued with Luke. When he got back to his feet, Luke told him to go for his gun. Luke wanted to get it settled once and for all. But the cowboy drawed back his fist and tried to slug Luke. Luke drawed his gun and shot him. Shot him twice, real fast. I never seen anything so fast. That cowboy never should have tangled with Luke."

Molly felt the pressure of her own pulse as blood pounded through her head. Her ears roared.

Cinnamon Sam said, "I ain't supposed to be talking about this to nobody. I done swore to Luke. If he knew I told, he'd kill me."

Molly said softly, "His killing days are over."

If Cinnamon Sam heard her, he did not understand her meaning. The little man's voice shook with fear when he repeated, "Please don't tell him."

"Don't worry about Standifer," Molly said. "All you have to worry about is going to bed. Now, climb that staircase. Don't look back, or you'll be looking at a bullet coming at you. Get into bed and stay there. Understand?"

Cinnamon Sam murmured, "Yes, ma'am."

Molly watched Cinnamon Sam go up the stairs. The steps creaked under his weight. When the swamper reached the top, he opened the door there and went inside, closing the door behind him.

Molly waited several minutes, then walked back out to Main Street. She edged her way along the boardwalk until she was across the street from the hotel. When she was certain no one was about, she ran to the door of the Liberty Hotel and entered the lobby.

In her room Molly undressed in the dark and changed into nightclothes. Only after she had climbed into bed and breathed deeply for several minutes could she calm herself. She was not frightened; she was excited. She had found what she had come for. Luke Standifer had murdered her brother. And there were two witnesses.

Chapter XVI

In Denver, Charley Castle bought five hundred dollars worth of gold dust. From a clerk in a mining supply company he learned of a miner in town who was known to have some rich samples of gold ore. Charley Castle located this man in a saloon and bought a dozen of his best samples. They ranged in size from a man's fist to a melon and were dramatically heavy. Charley Castle tactfully did not ask where the ore had come from.

At the mining-supply company Charley Castle purchased an ore wagon. He loaded this large, distinctive type of wagon with basic hard-rock mining tools: hand drills, single jacks, dynamite, blasting caps, fuses, precut mining timbers, and a wheelbarrow. From a liveryman he bought a mule team.

Before leaving Denver, Charley Castle made one last purchase: a double-barreled shotgun and ammunition. He took the gun to a blacksmith and had the barrel shortened to twelve inches. Then, with his ore wagon loaded on a flat car, Charley Castle boarded the northbound train. By afternoon he would be in Liberty.

After breakfast at Martha's Kitchen, Molly returned to the hotel and made light conversation with Nate Stiles. She mentioned that she had seen the Liberty Dance Hall and asked if he knew who owned the place.

"Sure, I do," he said. "Its owned by two sisters, middle-aged, by the name of June and April Rockwell." He studied Molly for a moment and asked, "You don't aim to go to work there, do you, Molly? That's a rough line of work for a lady."
he knew who owned the place.

Satisfied that Molly would not become a fallen dove, Nate Stiles told her all he knew about the Rockwells. June Rockwell was the boss. She was queen of the realm and dressed and acted the part. Her sister, April, was the opposite. April acted like a poor maid and was treated like one. Nate Stiles said she acted like a whupped hound.

Later in the morning Molly left the hotel and walked down Main to Second Street, then on to the dance hall. She was happy that she did not run into Luke Standifer. She wanted to avoid him, yet she could not hide in her room all day. She had to find Jennifer.

The Rockwell sisters and the girls who worked in the dance hall lived in the house next door, known locally as the Rockwell House. Molly had given the house only a passing glance when she had walked by yesterday. Now she looked at it closely. It had the appearance of a boardinghouse, two stories high, and was embraced by a stout fence of wrought-iron spikes.

Molly opened the gate and followed the walk to the screened porch. She twisted the bell handle in the door and heard it ring on the other side of the door. Because of Nate Stiles's apt description, she immediately recognized the dowdy woman who answered as April Rockwell.

"My name is Molly Castle. May I speak to June Rockwell?"

April nodded. She stepped aside, fixing her eyes somewhere near Molly's feet.

Molly entered a carpeted drawing room. She smiled at April, but failed to catch her eye. The woman looked as if she could use a smile this morning. She wore a baggy cotton dress that might have had a pattern once, heavy mail-order shoes, and her dull brown hair was tied in a small bun behind her head. April mumbled for Molly to be seated, then left the room, staring at the carpet as she walked.

Molly sat on the edge of an upholstered chair. The papered walls of the drawing room were decorated with framed pastel scenes of faraway, exotic lands. The scenes were like magic windows that permitted the viewer to see beyond the familiar rolling hill country of Liberty, Colorado.

Molly saw a family resemblance between the sisters when June Rockwell made her entrance into the drawing room. But there was no other resemblance. June Rockwell carried her head in a high and regal way. Her shining hair was piled high over her head in a fashionable design that might have attracted bees. The long, elegant dress she wore was trimmed with delicate lace, and she seemed to float into the drawing room, reminding Molly of the gentle flight of a butterfly—gentle yet purposeful.

Molly stood. Despite herself, she felt humbled before this woman. And June Rockwell caught Molly's instant of hesitation—perhaps she was accustomed to it—and spoke first:

"Do be seated. My sister tells me you are Molly Castle. Did she get the name right? Oh good, April did something right today. I presume you are here seeking employment. First, let me tell you what will be expected of you—"

Molly felt her face grow warm as she interrupted, "No, Mrs. Rockwell, I'm not—"

"*Miss* Rockwell."

"No, Miss Rockwell," Molly went on, "I'm not here looking for work. I'll be in town only a short time. I have come to speak to you about a personal matter."

June Rockwell drew her head up higher. "Oh? And what is the nature of this personal matter?" She added quickly, "I do hope this is not one of those nasty situations that might involve your husband with one of my girls."

Molly felt a rush of anger. "Hardly." She went on in a softer tone of voice, "This matter concerns a girl who worked for you until very recently. Her name was Jennifer."

"Jennifer Hayes?"

Molly did not know Jennifer's last name, but she nodded and said, "She left on short notice, I understand. Did she leave a forwarding address?"

"No . . . she did not," June Rockwell said carefully. "Why do you ask?"

Molly realized she was being dominated in this conversation and would have to do something to gain the lead. "This matter is an extremely delicate one, Miss Rockwell."

June Rockwell laughed with surprising harshness. "I assure you, I have seen just about every kind of delicate situation a woman can get herself into."

I'll bet you have, Molly thought. Aloud, she said, "This matter concerns other parties. I don't feel free to talk about it. I can promise you that my question about Jennifer's whereabouts will work to her benefit, not to her harm."

June Rockwell nodded once.

Molly took that to mean, *I understand, but I don't like it.* Molly said, "And I can tell you that this is a matter of extreme importance. I don't exaggerate when I say it is a matter of life and death."

That turned the balance in Molly's favor. June Rockwell lowered her head and returned to the level of mortals. "Oh, my. I do wish I could help you. Jennifer was here, of course, then she was gone—vanished. She told no one what her plans were. I went to some lengths to find out because she had some back salary coming to her. I don't like to lose any of my girls, but when I do, I certainly don't like to be in debt to them."

Molly nodded.

"As near as April and I could determine," June Rockwell said, "Jennifer left most of her personal belongings here. The only thing we were certain was missing was one of her uniforms. Perhaps you have seen them. They are bright red with the girl's monogram across the front in white lace. But the girls love to wear their own clothes when they go out, so I can't explain why Jennifer would take hers. But she was quite distraught at the time and probably was not thinking clearly."

"What happened just before she disappeared?" Molly asked. She wanted to hear June Rockwell's version of the incident.

"Jennifer was caught up in a love triangle," June Rockwell said. "We all knew of it, but we couldn't stop it. She was pursued by two men. Actually, she was pursued at one time or another by every man in Liberty, but I'm talking about two in particular. One was a young, handsome cowboy. The other was older and more aggressive. He is the town marshal. Perhaps you have seen him about town."

Molly nodded. She felt her throat grow tight and painful.

"All of us who knew Jennifer," June Rockwell said, "knew that she was terribly in love with the young cowboy. But the more she tried to discourage the marshal, the more attentive and demanding he became. Well, to shorten a long story, the young cowboy and the marshal got into a violent fight one night in front of the dance hall. Jennifer witnessed the killing of her young man. In the morning she was gone."

Molly's voice shook when she asked, "Did anyone else see the killing?"

"None of my girls saw it," June Rockwell said. "I know that for a fact because all the girls answered April's bed check that night except Jennifer. I must admit, I was prepared to reprimand her when she did return. But soon after I retired that night, I heard two gunshots." She paused. "April and I spent a bad night trying to comfort Jennifer. We failed, needless to say."

"What did Jennifer tell you that night?" Molly asked.

"That her young man had been murdered," June Rockwell said. "She said it repeatedly. Jennifer was so emotionally torn apart that she was almost delirious. I don't think she knew what she was saying. You see, Marshal Standifer swore that he was forced to shoot the young cowboy in self-defense."

"Twice?" Molly asked.

June Rockwell looked at Molly curiously. "Are you here on the young man's behalf?"

"All I can tell you," Molly said, "is that you could be of great help to me, and to Jennifer, if you mentioned this conversation to no one."

"Very well," June Rockwell said. "But when you do find Jennifer, please tell her to write to me and let me know where she is. I wish to send her back salary to her."

Molly said she would, then asked, "Were there any girls here Jennifer was particularly close to?"

"She shared a room with three girls," June Rockwell said thoughtfully. "Of the three, she was closest to Mabel."

"May I speak to her?"

"It is early for my girls now," June Rockwell said. "Perhaps you could return this evening—shortly after the dinner hour?"

"I will," Molly said, standing. "Thank you for your help."

"I hope you find Jennifer soon," June Rockwell said. She crossed the room with Molly and opened the door.

"So do I," Molly said. She thanked June Rockwell again, and left.

Molly was deep in her thoughts as she walked up Second Street toward Main. She knew more about Jennifer now than she had before, but she had learned nothing that would help her locate the girl. She hoped Mabel would have an idea where Jennifer had gone.

As Molly rounded the corner at Main, she caught a glimpse of a man behind her. She glanced back and immediately wished she hadn't. Luke Standifer was following her.

Chapter XVII

Molly's first impulse was to run. The faceless man from her nightmare was coming after her, and she must escape. But Molly held her fear in check. She stopped and turned to meet Standifer.

When Standifer caught up, he touched his hand to the brim of his Stetson. "Good morning, Mrs. Castle. Been visiting the Rockwells?"

Molly nodded and tried to smile.

"I didn't know you were a friend of theirs," he said.

Molly wondered if she heard suspicion in his voice or imagined it. "I'm not. I was there to ask after my husband."

"Oh," Standifer said slowly. "Well, did June Rockwell know where Charley Castle is?"

"No, she didn't," Molly said. She added, "And I asked her not to tell anyone I had inquired about him."

"I know June Rockwell," Standifer said. "Your secret's safe with her. With me, too."

Molly nodded in reply.

Standifer glanced down Main, then looked back at Molly.

"Why don't you have dinner with me? There's a good cafe down the street."

"I can't," Molly said quickly. She looked around, searching for a believable reason, and saw Benson's Livery. "Bess Tanner is expecting me. I have to go now."

Standifer's brow knotted. He looked frustrated, almost angered. "Mrs. Castle, maybe you think I'm just a town marshal. Maybe you think I ain't got much future. Well, I own land north of here, plenty of it. When the railroad goes through, I'll be a rich man. I aim to raise horses in this country someday. I got a good future." He fell silent, then said, "I want you to think good of me. You're better than any other women I've known. You're a real lady."

Molly was surprised at this outpouring from Standifer. She realized he was on the verge of making a proposal to her.

"I must leave now, Marshal," she said.

Standifer nodded reluctantly. "I'll keep on hunting for Charley Castle. You can depend on me."

The afternoon train brought Charley Castle back to Liberty. After his ore wagon was off-loaded from the train's flat car, he hooked up his mule team and drove the big wagon from the depot to the Silver Dollar Saloon.

The men who lounged in the shade in front of the saloon watched with great curiosity. Inside there was a brief commotion as men came to the window and swing doors to look at what was probably the only ore wagon in that part of Colorado.

Charley Castle climbed down from the high seat. He made his way through the knot of onlookers and entered the saloon, aware that every man there was watching him. At the bar he was greeted loudly, and drunkenly, by Melvin Goodwin. Charley Castle joined him.

In a voice that was meant to be a whisper, but wasn't, Goodwin said, "I had a suspicion you were planning to open a mine, Mr. Tucker. You saw something out there on that quarter section, didn't you?"

Charley Castle ordered rye whiskey from the smiling bartender. "You're right, Mr. Goodwin. I did see something."

"To my mind," Goodwin said happily, "we're partners. I own the property."

"That's true enough," Charley Castle said.

"Well," Goodwin asked, "are you on to something big?"

"I don't know yet," Charley Castle said. "Mining is a gamble."

"I like gambles," Goodwin said. "Especially when a man like you is doing the gambling. You know what you're doing."

"I hope so," Charley Castle said.

Charley Castle had almost finished his drink when Standifer came into the saloon. Goodwin greeted him loudly, but the marshal ignored him and walked to a table where a lone gambler sat.

Goodwin was embarrassed at being ignored. His face was flushed as he turned away. That was the moment Charley Castle heard his real name spoken by Standifer—not the Tucker name.

"Where was he when you seen him last?"

Through the mirror Charley Castle saw Standifer leaning over the gambler. The gambler pursed his lips thoughtfully.

"Colorado Springs."

"That was last winter," Standifer said. "You ain't seen him since then?"

Charley Castle watched the gambler shake his head. Standifer straightened up, looked around the saloon, and walked out.

Charley Castle drank a silent toast to the gambler, and then another to the lady in the forest. He did not know for certain how Standifer had got on his trail, but he suspected the lady he needed to ask was named Molly.

He was aware that Melvin Goodwin was speaking to him again in that hoarse voice that was intended to be a whisper.

"Luke Standifer doesn't know about the big deal I made on

that quarter section he sold me. He'd show some respect for me if he knew. You don't mind my telling him about the lease, do you, Mr. Tucker?"

Even as he thought of Standifer's questioning of the gambler, Charley Castle knew he had gone too far to stop the course of the events he had set in motion.

"No, I don't mind, Mr. Goodwin." Charley Castle declined the bartender's offer to refill his glass and left the Silver Dollar Saloon.

On the way to the Circle 7 Ranch, Molly tried to think away her nagging worries. Had Standifer been following her because he was suspicious of her, or was it only chance that he was in that part of town? What if he talked to June Rockwell? What if Cinnamon Sam, accidentally or purposely, told what happened to him in the alley that night?

Standifer might not be an intelligent man, but Molly had no doubt that he was shrewd and his instincts were animal-sharp. If he had a suspicion, he would follow it to its logical end. That meant he might well be talking to June Rockwell before long. Even if she gave him only a vague account of their talk, Standifer would know he was on to something.

Molly weighed these speculations in her mind and tried to foresee the consequences of imagined events. She got nowhere. Restless, and exasperated with these nagging worries, Molly urged the horse to a canter the rest of the way to the Circle 7 Ranch.

In the log house Bess had gathered up Chick's belongings on a table.

"Everything's here, Molly, except his saddle and horse. His saddle is out in the tack room. And that horse of his is out in the south pasture, getting fat. Chick's clothes are here, his fancy pocket watch, and that Barlow knife he always carried. He had a savings account in the bank, too. I reckon you won't be claiming that until you start using your own name again, will you?"

Molly shook her head in reply as she idly sorted through

Chick's belongings: light cotton shirts, well-worn denim trousers, chaps, a pair of spurs that jingled when Molly picked them up, a revolver and holster, several red bandanna handkerchiefs, one pair of boots that were run down at the heels.

Smiling, Molly picked up the Barlow knife. Their father had carried one. It pleased Molly to know that Chick had continued this small tradition.

"How are things going in town, Molly?"

"I've learned a few things," Molly said. "Now I have to find that dance hall girl, Jennifer Hayes."

"Why?" Bess asked.

"She was a witness to Chick's murder."

"Murder?" Bess said. "Can you prove that?"

"Not yet," Molly said. She told Bess about her talks with Cinnamon Sam and with June Rockwell.

"Well, you are a top-notch investigator," Bess said.

"I'm still a long ways off from having enough evidence to satisfy a jury," Molly said.

"How are you going to find Jennifer?" Bess asked.

"I wish I knew," Molly said. "This evening I'll talk to one of the dance hall girls who knew her. If she can't help me, I don't know what I'll do."

Molly picked up Chick's pocket watch, wound it, and held it to her ear.

"I thought that looked like a family heirloom," Bess said.

"It belonged to Father," Molly said. She looked down at the table. "This watch and that Barlow knife are all I want to keep, Bess. I want you to take the rest of his belongings."

"Oh, I couldn't," Bess said. "Chick paid over fifty dollars for his saddle. I don't know what he paid for his horse, but it must have been plenty. He wanted a good one, and Barney helped him pick one out. You won't have any trouble selling that horse."

Molly put the Barlow knife and watch into the buttoned pocket of her riding skirt. "I have a better idea: why don't you give that horse and saddle to Barney?"

Bess argued until she saw that Molly had made up her mind. "Barney will be thrilled clean to his toes. He's always had a liking for that horse."

"That's fine," Molly said.

Bess took her by the arm. "Come on outside. I want you to help me do some work."

Behind the house Bess grabbed up a hoe and a spade and walked up the slope toward the aspen grove. Molly realized what the older woman wanted to do. Molly almost turned back, but then she followed Bess to the fenced burial ground.

Molly and Bess dug weeds that had grown up over all the graves but Chick's. They smoothed the soil and placed small stones around Chick's grave in a decorative way. All the while Bess maintained a steady stream of talk, reminiscing about her family.

Molly found the work to be curiously satisfying. When finished, she felt pleasantly tired and calm as though an obligation had been fulfilled.

Molly left the ranch in the afternoon. When she had climbed up into the saddle, Bess stepped off the front porch and looked up at her.

"You be careful, Molly," she said, "mighty careful."

Molly smiled down at her. "I will."

As Molly rode out of the yard, Bess called out in a stern voice, "And don't you forget to come back!"

Charley Castle had not worked as a miner since first coming to Colorado as a young man in the 1870s. In those days of his youth he had dreams of making a big strike, instantly becoming rich, and living out a life of ease and luxury and world travel.

But Charley Castle soon learned that hard-rock mining meant long hours of strenuous work. A miner's working life was spent in darkness. He went underground early in the morning and came out in the evening. Charley Castle came to a realization in those days that escaped many other young men: the odds of making any kind of strike, much less a big one, were slim. Over the years Charley Castle had found easier and surer ways of making money.

He drove his new ore wagon down the JD road and turned off on the pair of wagon ruts that cut through the meadow. He crested the hill and drove down into Goodwin's meadow. Crossing the small stream, he drove on to the granite out-cropping.

Charley Castle set to work drilling a series of blasting holes near the base of the outcropping. He discovered he had lost his knack for hand drilling into solid rock, and the work went slowly and clumsily. When he finished, he had two blackened fingernails, an open blister on his palm, and a deep scrape across the back of one hand to show for his labor.

Moving his team and wagon a safe distance away from the outcropping, he loaded the holes with sticks of dynamite. The sticks were impregnated with blasting caps which in turn were crimped to fuses. After lighting a master fuse, he ran back to his wagon, yelling, "Fire in the hole! Fire in the hole!"

The explosion was deafening. The entire meadow and hill-side were showered with chunks of granite ranging in size from thimbles to watermelons. Charley Castle picked himself up off the ground. He couldn't recall if he had dived to the earth, or had been thrown there by the concussion of the blast. He calmed his mule team by promising to use a lighter charge next time.

Charley Castle walked back to the outcropping and sur-veyed the damage. A large, irregular hole had been opened into the base of the rock. Cracks had been opened. These would be much easier to drill into than solid rock. He picked up his drill and single jack and began drilling another series of holes.

The second blast was smaller, but achieved a result Charley Castle had hoped for. A white-haired man on a horse came charging over the hillside. As he came galloping across the meadow, Charley Castle heard him swearing.

Though he had seen Dundee only once before, in the Silver Dollar Saloon, Charley Castle recognized him now. For a man pushing seventy, Dundee moved well. Charley Castle watched him yank the galloping horse to a halt and jump out of the saddle, landing on both feet. His right hand brought an old revolver out of the hard leather holster on his hip.

"Mister, I'm giving you the count of ten to climb up on that big wagon and haul your butt out of here."

"Count as far as you can," Charley Castle said. "I'm not leaving."

"The hell," Dundee said. "If you're still on my land after the count of ten, you'll be leaving feet first."

"This isn't your land," Charley Castle said.

Justin Dundee's anger made him fight for words. "I've been here since the fall of '60, mister. Who the hell are you to tell me this ain't my land?"

"You sold it," Charley Castle said. "I saw the deed myself."

"I sold it to a man who's going to raise horses here," Dundee said. "There wasn't nothing said about some stranger coming in here and blowing the land to hell."

"Standifer sold this quarter section to a speculator," Charley Castle said. "I took a sixty-day lease on it to do some exploratory mining."

"Sold it?" Dundee exclaimed. "He wasn't supposed to sell this land. . . ." The old rancher's voice trailed off. He lowered his revolver, then holstered it.

"I don't know what agreement you had with Standifer about this land," Charley Castle said. "The current owner placed no restrictions on how I use it."

Justin Dundee shook his head slowly. "The hell."

Charley Castle watched him catch his horse, step up into the saddle with surprising ease, and gallop back across the meadow and over the far hill. It was a safe bet, Charley Castle thought, that Dundee would ride straight for town.

Charley Castle walked back to his wagon and brought out his sawed-off shotgun and a box of ammunition. He opened the ends of two twelve-gauge shells and poured out the shot.

Taking out a leather pouch of placer gold from his pocket, he poured about two ounces into each shell, then closed the ends and loaded them into the shotgun. Aiming point blank at the back wall of the tunnel, he fired first one barrel, then the other.

Charley Castle returned to his wagon and pried the lid off a wooden crate. Inside were the specimens of high-grade gold ore he had bought from the miner in Denver. He carried the crate back to the mine and spread the gold on the tunnel floor. He stirred his foot around in the debris, mixing the gold specimens in.

Charley Castle stepped back and examined his work. The back wall of granite was covered with gold. The ore samples on the floor appeared to have been brought down by the dynamite blast. Only an experienced miner would recognize this as a salted mine. To a novice, as most miners were even in a mining region, this was a bonanza.

As Charley Castle walked back to his wagon, his eye caught movement on the far hillside. At first he thought Justin Dundee had returned. But he looked again and saw the man drop back and disappear behind the hill. He was not Dundee. For he appeared to have long hair and a shaggy beard.

Charley Castle got into his wagon and headed back for town. While he had no idea who the man was, he was not worried about him. Other men might find this mine. If they were fooled by it, it was all to the better. If not, then he knew he would have no chance of deceiving Luke Standifer.

Chapter XVIII

At sundown Molly returned to the Rockwell House. June Rockwell sent her sister upstairs after Mabel. Then June Rockwell excused herself, saying she must prepare mind and body for the evening's work.

April brought Mabel into the drawing room and introduced her to Molly. Mabel, a lean, attractive woman, wore her Rockwell uniform. It was a long, bright red dress with her initials emblazoned across the front in white.

Mabel knew very little about Jennifer's background. She recalled Jennifer once saying she was an orphan who had run away from the orphanage at the age of fourteen. She had worked in several dance halls in Denver before coming to Liberty a year ago. In answer to Molly's question, Mabel said as far as she knew Jennifer had neither sent nor received any letters as long as she had been here.

Molly asked Mabel if she thought Jennifer was in love with Luke Standifer. Mabel shook her head quickly, then looked embarrassed. Molly was surprised at the reaction, but did not know what it meant.

After Mabel went back upstairs, April showed Molly to the front door. As Molly stepped through the doorway, she had a new thought. Of all the women here, quiet April might know more of what went on in the Rockwell House than anyone.

"April, is there anything you can tell me about Jennifer? It's extremely important."

April glanced at Molly, then looked away. "No."

"I need all the help I can get," Molly said.

After a long silence April said softly, "I don't know any more than June does."

"Ordinarily, I wouldn't ask anyone to repeat gossip," Molly said. "But it is important that I know as much about Jennifer as I can learn. I need some clue as to where she might have gone. Anything you tell me will be held in confidence."

For a moment April looked into Molly's eyes and she seemed ready to speak. But then she caught herself and remained silent.

Molly asked, "You trust me, don't you?"

April nodded.

Molly sensed she would get nowhere here. The mood of June Rockwell's dominance hung over this house like a dark cloud.

"I'm returning to my room at the Liberty Hotel now," Molly said. "If you think of anything that might help me in my search for Jennifer, will you come and tell me?"

April nodded. Her lower lip quivered as her deepest emotions threatened to boil over. She said nothing and avoided Molly's eyes.

Molly stepped out to the porch. "Good night, April."

April closed the door.

Molly walked back toward Main, passing by the gaudy front of the Liberty Dance Hall. She wondered if she had done the right thing. Perhaps if she had assumed June's role and demanded April answer her questions, she would have got some answers. Molly was certain April had some ideas about Jennifer's whereabouts. And Molly suspected she could explain Mabel's curious reaction to the mention of Luke Standifer's name.

Molly followed the boardwalk down Main Street to the train depot. She found the window of the telegraph office there and wired the city marshal's office in Denver:

SEEK WHEREABOUTS OF JENNIFER HAYES FEMALE
STOP EMPLOYED IN DANCE HALLS IN DENVER UNTIL
ONE YEAR AGO STOP YOUNG PRETTY NO OTHER
DESCRIPTION STOP RETURN FINDINGS TO LIBERTY
HOTEL, MOLLY OWENS, FENTON OPERATIVE 23 STOP

It was a long shot, but one she had to try now. If the inquiry proved to be a dead end, she would have to go back to the Rockwell House. She could question April again, and perhaps Mabel, too.

Now Molly's theory of a link between the trial of Bess Tanner and the murder of her brother seemed to hold no promise. She had uncovered no evidence to support the theory. Bess's firm belief that Justin Dundee would have no part in hiring Standifer to kill a man appeared to be accurate. All the evidence now pointed to an ancient killer: a love triangle.

Molly saw Justin Dundee for the first time when she returned to the hotel. She was building up to taking Nate Stiles into her confidence when he pointed out the window.

"There's a man you don't see in town often these days," he said.

Molly looked to the street outside. A white-haired man on

a lathered horse rode past. The horse pranced excitedly. The rider, sitting straight in the saddle, held a tight rein and looked intently from one boardwalk to the other. Molly asked who he was.

"Justin Dundee," Nate Stiles said. "Years ago, he was top dog in these parts. He called most of the shots. But when Liberty got bigger, folks saw Dundee for what he was: a rancher, not a king. Nowadays, Dundee mostly stays out on the JD. Out there he is king, I reckon. I wonder who he's looking for?"

They soon found out. From the hotel window they watched Justin Dundee tie his sweating horse at the rail in front of the Silver Dollar Saloon. He punched through the batwing doors and left them swinging violently behind him.

In a short time Dundee came back through the doors, followed by two men. To Molly's great surprise, one was Standifer. The second, a pudgy man wearing a derby hat cocked on his head, was identified by Nate Stiles as a speculator who lived here in the hotel. His name was Melvin Goodwin.

"Looks like a parley," Nate Stiles observed.

Molly smiled as she caught the understatement of his remark. Standifer and Dundee were obviously arguing. Dundee repeatedly jabbed his finger into Standifer's chest. Standifer brushed it away angrily. Melvin Goodwin kept a safe distance from the two men.

The argument appeared to climax, then end. Justin Dundee untied his horse and stepped up into the saddle. He said a few parting words to Standifer, then came riding back up the street at a canter. Molly watched him pass by, then looked back at the saloon. Standifer went inside. Goodwin followed.

Now Molly's suspicions of Standifer and Dundee were rekindled. She asked Nate Stiles if the two were friends.

"I don't know," he said. "I know they're both interested in raising horses. But like I told you, Dundee hardly ever comes to town any more." He added thoughtfully, "Except during the trial with Bess Tanner. He was in town quite a bit then."

That was what Molly was thinking, too.

"Nate," Molly said, "I have something to tell you. I'm going to have to ask you to keep it secret."

Nate Stiles grinned. "What kind of secret would you have, Molly?"

Molly reached into her handbag and brought out her Fenton identification card. She handed it to him.

Nate Stiles was surprised. "You from the Fentons? What are you doing here?"

"I can't tell you," Molly said. "I'm making an investigation here. It's important that no one knows about it."

"Well, I won't tell anybody," Nate Stiles said. "But why are you telling me?"

"Because I know I can trust you," Molly said. "In the next day or two I should be getting a telegram from Denver. It will have my real name on it: Molly Owens. Will you hold that telegram for me?"

"You bet I will," Nate Stiles said. "I hope you'll tell me what this is all about someday."

"I will," Molly said. "And soon, I hope."

Nate Stiles grinned toothlessly. "This is real inter-esting."

Charley Castle drove his ore wagon back to Liberty. He was in sight of the houses on the edge of town when Justin Dundee galloped past. Dundee must have recognized Charley Castle, but he gave no sign.

Charley Castle left his mule team and wagon at Benson's. He went to his hotel room. He had been there only a few minutes when he heard a soft knock on his door. He opened it.

"I've been looking for you," Molly said.

Charley Castle let her in and closed the door behind her. "Have you arrested Luke Standifer yet?"

Molly ignored the question and told what she had learned from Cinnamon Sam and June Rockwell. In conclusion she said as soon as she found Jennifer she would be ready to press charges against Standifer.

"I could press charges now," Molly said, "but I know Cinnamon Sam would not be a dependable witness." She went on to tell him how she had urged Cinnamon Sam to tell her what he knew.

Charley Castle shook his head. Then he said, "I hear Standifer's hunting a confidence man named Charley Castle."

Molly felt her face grow hot. She had almost forgotten the wild story she had stumbled into when she had first talked to Standifer. She sat down and repeated it now.

"Look what civilization has come to," Charley Castle said.

Molly apologized, then said cheerfully, "He's looking for a bearded, older man. He'll never figure out who you are."

"Beware of a woman's praise," Charley Castle said.

Hoping to change the subject, Molly said, "This evening I saw Standifer talking to Justin Dundee. They were arguing about something. I'm beginning to think they're in cahoots, after all."

Charley Castle said he knew what the argument was about.

"You do?" Molly asked. "How?"

Charley Castle gave a brief account of his activities since he had last seen her. Molly was amazed and demanded to know what he was up to.

"Exploratory mining," Charley Castle said.

"Tell me!" Molly said, suddenly angry. "You know this is important to me."

"I'm taking advantage of the opportunities," Charley Castle said.

Molly realized he would say no more about his scheme. "I think I'll have a talk with Justin Dundee tomorrow."

"If you poke your derringer into that man's ear," Charley Castle said, "he'll bite your head off and spit down your windpipe."

"I can handle him," Molly said.

"No, you can't," Charley Castle said.

Molly stood up. She was about to reply when she heard the scuff of a boot heel out in the hallway. In the next moment there was a loud knock on the door.

"Who's there?" Charley Castle asked.

"Luke Standifer."

Frightened now, Molly looked at Charley Castle. Then they both glanced around the room and saw what they already knew to be true. There were no hiding places, not even a clothes closet.

"Just a minute," Charley Castle said, motioning for Molly to drop to the floor and get under the bed.

Molly sank to her hands and knees and flattened out and crawled under the bed. The bedspread was several inches short of reaching the floor. It was light under the bed, and Molly felt no comfort of concealment. She pressed her arms to her sides and tried to make herself small. Charley Castle opened the door.

"Good evening, Marshal. What can I do for you?"

"Howdy, Mr. Tucker," Standifer said. "I found out where you was staying from a man named Melvin Goodwin. I believe you know him."

"I've leased a quarter section from him," Charley Castle said.

"I know about that quarter section," Standifer said. "I'm the man who sold it to Goodwin. It used to be part of the JD Ranch. I reckon you already know that."

"How does it concern you, Marshal?" Charley Castle asked. "That's out of your jurisdiction, I believe."

"I'm only the town marshal," Standifer admitted. "The county sheriff is on the other side of the mountains. But it's up to me to know what's going on around here."

"You seem to," Charley Castle said.

Standifer took that as a compliment and smiled. "Well, I know you're doing some mining on that quarter section. And I know Dundee is hot to file a complaint against you. He says you've spooked his cattle by setting off dynamite. He's ready to go to the county seat and file a complaint."

"Let him," Charley Castle said. "I'm within my rights."

"I reckon you're right," Standifer said. "But Dundee told me he aims to close off his road to you."

Now Charley Castle took on a troubled expression. "I have to have access to the mine."

"That's what I wanted to talk to you about," Standifer said.

"About Dundee?" Charley Castle asked.

"I want to know what you're finding in that mine," Standifer said.

Charley Castle shook his head.

"Well, if you ain't finding ore," Standifer said, "it don't matter to me, one way or the other. Dundee will close off that ranch road. But if you are finding some ore, I'll see that you get the use of that road."

"How can you do that?" Charley Castle asked.

"Don't worry over that," Standifer said. "I can do it. Now, what are you finding on that quarter section?"

Molly listened intently as Charley Castle fell silent. At last she heard him say: "All right, Marshal. Step in here and take a look at this."

Charley Castle lifted his carpet bag from the floor to the bed. He had placed the most valuable samples of gold ore inside. He opened the bag and showed them to Standifer.

"Gold," Standifer whispered. Aloud, he asked, "You took this ore out of that hillside up there?"

Charley Castle nodded. "Don't tell anyone. I don't want a stampede."

Standifer examined the other samples of gold. "I've worked in mining camps, Mr. Tucker. I don't know much about mines, but I know gold when I see it. This ore is as rich as any I've seen."

"It appears to be a good deposit," Charley Castle said casually. He looked at Standifer as the marshal held a heavy specimen of gold near the lamplight. Standifer did not need to say what was on his mind. Charley Castle could almost see his thoughts at that moment: *Why the hell did I ever sell that quarter section?*

Standifer laid the gold back on the bed. "I'll tell Dundee to let you use that road."

"He didn't strike me as a man who could be told anything he didn't want to hear," Charley Castle said.

"He'll listen to me," Standifer said, "if he knows you and me are partners."

Charley Castle took on an expression of surprise. "How much of a partnership are you thinking about?"

"Half," Standifer said.

"No," Charley Castle said, shaking his head. "That's too big a bite."

"Without me," Standifer said, "you won't take an ounce of gold off that quarter section."

Charley Castle started to protest. Then he said, "I'm over a barrel."

"I'm just the man to get you off that barrel," Standifer said.

"Are you sure you can talk Dundee into letting me use that road?" Charley Castle asked.

"I can do it," Standifer said impatiently. "Do we have a deal, or don't we?"

"I don't have much choice," Charley Castle said. "We have a deal."

"You're a smart man," Standifer said. "Tomorrow morning I'll get a legal document drawed up, and we'll sign it. Then we'll ride out to the JD."

Molly saw the feet of the two men as they moved to the door. She heard Standifer say:

"We'll keep this partnership secret, Mr. Tucker, from everybody."

"That's all right by me," Charley Castle said.

When Standifer had gone and Charley Castle had closed the door behind him, Molly crawled out from under the bed. She stood, brushing dust and lint from her dress front.

"What are you up to, Charley Castle?"

"Taking advantage of the opportunities," he said. "Stay away from Dundee for now, Molly. I may want you to talk to him later."

Molly nodded. "All right. I wish I knew what you were doing."

"I'm trying to help you," Charley Castle said.

"When I came here, I thought I didn't need your help," Molly said. "But I was wrong."

Charley Castle smiled and moved close to her. "Look what civilization has come to now."

Chapter XIX

In the morning Charley Castle met Luke Standifer in a lawyer's office on the second floor of the bank building. They drew up and signed a document giving each an equal partnership in the gold mine. For legal purposes, the mine had to be named. Charley Castle could hardly suppress his smile when Standifer made an immediate suggestion.

"We'll call it the Molly Mine," he said.

Charley Castle agreed to the name and signed the copies of the document. Then he and Standifer left town and rode to the headquarters of the JD Ranch.

Justin Dundee, hatless, met them on his front porch. He did not invite either man to step down. Instead Dundee stood with his hands on his hips as he looked from one man to the other, and he threw a scornful glance at the outsized wagon Charley Castle drove.

"Yesterday I told you how things set," Dundee said. He jerked his head at Charley Castle, but went on speaking to Standifer. "I won't have this man crossing my land."

"I reckon you'll let him," Standifer said. He added, "I rode out here myself to look at his mine."

"Mine, hell," Dundee said, waving a hand at Charley Castle. "If he don't stay off this ranch, he'll be mining six feet under."

"Mr. Tucker's a gee-ologist from Chicago," Standifer said. "He has a legal right to open a mine on that quarter section."

"I don't care if he dropped out of the sky on a white horse," Dundee said loudly. "He ain't crossing the JD."

Standifer said, "Calm down, Mr. Dundee."

Now Justin Dundee pointed his finger at Standifer as though it were a loaded gun. "I've ranched here for thirty years, better'n thirty years. The JD is grassland, always has been. Always will be, too. I won't set still for any man who comes in here and dynamites the land and scares hell out of my stock. I've got cows scattered from here to hell and gone. You wasn't supposed to sell that land, Standifer. You told me you wanted to raise horses—"

"Now, Mr. Dundee," Standifer began.

"To hell with this palaver!" Dundee shouted. "Get off my ranch, both of you!"

Suddenly Standifer smiled. Charley Castle's glance went from the marshal to the old rancher. Dundee's white forehead, in contrast to his weather-tanned face, turned crimson as he stared at Standifer. Charley Castle saw a silent but strong communication pass between the two men, and in that moment he learned a thing about them that neither man would ever have told him. Standifer had a hold on this old man.

While matching Dundee's stare, Standifer said calmly, "Mr. Tucker, why don't you go on down to the mine? I'll catch up."

Charley Castle turned the wagon and drove slowly along the ranch road toward the set of tracks that cut through the pasture land. Behind, he heard the flat, commanding voice of Standifer, but could not hear his words. Dundee's reply was louder.

"You're an evil man, Standifer. Evil and greedy."

Charley Castle had topped the hill and was crossing the meadow when Standifer overtook him. He rode alongside, but said nothing. They crossed the willow-choked stream and continued on to the granite outcropping.

Charley Castle stopped the wagon near the mouth of the small tunnel. He climbed down and watched Standifer. The marshal had dismounted and walked to the mine. He swore reverently as he touched the gold imbedded in the granite rock. Now in the sunlight of late morning the gold shone brilliantly yellow, not sparkling and brassy like fool's gold, but intense in color and exciting.

Standifer backed out of the short tunnel. "I've heard of discoveries like this, but I've never seen one. What do you reckon this mine's worth, Tucker?"

"There's no way of knowing," Charley Castle said. "This is only the beginning."

Standifer shook his head in pleasant disbelief as though this mine was too good to be true. His glance went to the tunnel floor. He dug his toe into the loose rock there, then stooped down. He picked up a sample of gold ore the size of a small apple.

Charley Castle watched him and said, "Mr. Dundee sounded like he was in no mood to change his mind about the road."

"He changed his mind," Standifer said as he studied the heavy ore sample. Then, as if to explain, he went on, "I talked sense to him. Old Dundee's a mighty smart man. He'll listen to sense."

Charley Castle picked up a short drill and his single jack. He placed the drill in a crack in the rock, and struck it with the hammer. By turning the drill slightly after each stroke, he began hand drilling a hole in the granite. Because the dynamite blast had made a crack, the work went faster now. The single jack slammed against the drill rapidly, making sounds like small gunshots.

Charley Castle raised up in time to see Standifer put the ore sample into his trouser pocket. "I wouldn't advise you to be showing that high-grade ore around town. You'll start a gold rush."

Standifer smiled. "I've worked in mining camps all through the Colorado Rockies, Mr. Tucker. I know the makings of a stampede when I see them." He paused and added, "There's only one person in Liberty who'll see this ore."

"Who's that," Charley Castle asked, "a lady?"

Suspicion clouded Standifer's face. "What made you say that?"

"Just a guess," Charley Castle said lightly. "I hear you're quite a man with the ladies."

Standifer said, "The lady I aim to show this gold to is different from the kind you're talking about. She's a real lady."

Charley Castle went back to his work. Standifer caught his horse and swung up into the saddle. He rode close to Charley Castle.

"Goodwin don't know about this gold strike, does he?"

Charley Castle raised up. "No, he doesn't. Not yet."

"Don't tell him," Standifer said.

"All right," Charley Castle said. "But I can't keep him from looking. He owns the land."

"Not for long, he won't," Standifer said, turning his horse.

Charley Castle watched him kick his mount and gallop across the meadow and then up the hillside across the way. Standifer and Dundee were ripe. They could easily be brought to a confrontation. The question was when.

At noon Nate Stiles brought a telegram to Molly's room. The message was brief and disappointing. A check of Denver's saloons and dance halls by deputies of the city marshal had shown that no one named Jennifer Hayes was there now.

Discouraged, Molly tried to think what she could do now. She was weighing the possibility of talking to Justin Dundee after all when she heard a knock on her door. She opened it, hoping to find Charley Castle.

"I hope I ain't disturbing you," Luke Standifer said.

Molly felt a wave of disappointment wash over her. She shook her head. An uncomfortable moment passed as Standifer waited to be invited into Molly's room. When he understood she would not invite him in, he reached into his trouser pocket and brought out the sample of gold ore. He handed it to her.

"I'm celebrating today," he said.

"What is it?" Molly asked.

"It's gold," Standifer said. "Ain't you ever seen gold before?"

"Not like this," Molly said.

"That's how it looks when it comes out of a mine," Standifer said, taking the sample back. "And there's plenty more of it, too. I own the property it's on. Just this afternoon I traded a drunk speculator out of that mine property. I gave him some railroad land in trade. What do you reckon I named that gold mine?"

Molly shrugged.

"The Molly Mine," Standifer said. "What do you think of that?"

"I'm . . . surprised," she said.

"I thought you would be," Standifer said. "I aim to quit my marshaling job. I've been planning to quit for a long time. That's why I've been buying up investment land. I figured when the railroad came through, I'd sell out. Then I'd have enough money to start a horse ranch. But now I won't have to wait for the damned railroad. My gold mine will make me rich in a hurry."

Molly found she could not look into Standifer's face. She knew what he was building up to, but she did not know how to stop him.

"Maybe this is too sudden," Standifer went on, "but I'm asking you to throw in with me. Marry me, Molly. I'll make life easy for you. You're a fine lady. You're better than other women I know. I'll give you everything you could ever want, Molly. And I mean everything."

Molly looked down at the floor between them and shook her head.

"You think on it," Standifer said. "I know this is sudden, but you think of the good life you'll have from now on. Think of all the things you'll be able to buy yourself."

"No," Molly said. "I can't."

After a long silence, Standifer demanded, "What's the matter? Ain't I good enough for you?"

Molly grew dizzy. She wanted to shout the truth at him. But she tried to calm herself. "I'm a married woman."

"Castle run off from you," Standifer said impatiently. "There's no telling how many other women like you he's run off from. He's long gone. And he ain't likely to show up here. Liberty ain't his kind of town."

Standifer must have realized he was shouting. He lowered

his voice and went on, "I'll give you the money Castle stole from your family. How much was it?"

Molly felt sick and feverish. She could hardly keep herself from screaming, *You killed my brother!*

"I reckon you don't know what this means to me," Standifer said. "I've worked around gold and silver camps for years. I've seen men that were dirt poor one day get rich overnight. They was lucky, that's all. Well, now I got lucky. And you're the finest lady I've ever known. Don't you see what this means to me now?"

Molly nodded. She did understand, and, for a moment, she pitied the man.

"Well," Standifer said at last, "I know this is sudden, Molly. You think on what I said. I'll come back later and we'll talk some more."

Molly closed the door. She crossed the room and sat on her bed, feeling weak and sick to her stomach. Coming to Liberty on the train, she had thought everything would be easy. All she had to do was gain Standifer's confidence, then trick him into confessing the murder of Chick Owens. As a Fenton investigator, she had tricked other men. But somehow this was different. The perfect opportunity was here, but she could not go through with it.

Molly lay back on the bed. She felt now as she had felt in the Brown Palace Hotel when she had first learned of Chick's death. Her life had reached an end. She had no family left. She had no man. And now the final irony was that the man who desperately wanted to marry her was the man who had murdered her brother.

Early that evening Molly heard a soft knock on her door. She opened it slowly, at once hoping to find Charley Castle and fearing she would find Luke Standifer.

"Hello, Molly," April Rockwell said.

"April!" Molly exclaimed. "This is a pleasant surprise. Come in."

April glanced down the hall nervously. "I can't stay." She looked back at Molly. "I know why you're in Liberty. I'm frightened."

"Why?" Molly asked. "What's happened?"

"Marshal Standifer was in our house," April said. "Mabel is one of his lady friends, and he wanted to see her. They went away together, but then they came back. Marshal Standifer was very angry. He shouted at June and me. He wanted to know all about you."

"Did June tell him what we had talked about?" Molly asked.

April nodded. "He threatened us. He's a bad man."

Molly took a deep breath and tried to control the fear that surged through her. "How long ago was he there?"

"About half an hour ago," April said. She paused as she looked thoughtfully at Molly. "You're here because of that young cowboy, aren't you?"

Molly nodded. "How did you know?"

"You look enough like him to be related to him," April said. "You think the marshal murdered him, don't you? And you think Jennifer can prove it."

"You're right," Molly said.

April shook her head. "I'm frightened."

"Why?" Molly asked. "What do you know about Jennifer?"

"I don't know anything," April said. "Only I feel something."

"What?" Molly asked, hearing her own voice grow shrill.

April's lips quivered as her emotions welled up inside her. "I don't think Jennifer . . . Jennifer ever got away from him. . . ." Tears choked off her voice. April brushed a hand across her eyes, then whirled and ran down the hallway to the stairs.

Molly did not follow. Time was short now. Standifer had learned all he needed to know from Mabel and the Rockwells. His next move would be in Molly's direction. Her hands shook violently as she changed into her riding clothes.

Molly descended the stairs and walked through the empty lobby. Nate Stiles was not in his chair beside the desk. She found him outside by the front door, watching a crowd of townspeople that had gathered in front of the Silver Dollar Saloon.

"Don't go down there, Molly," Nate Stiles said.

Molly looked down the street. People were crowded around a blanket-covered shape on the ground.

"What happened?" Molly asked.

"They just brung Cinnamon Sam down from his room," Nate Stiles said. "He's deader than hell. I seen him myself. The whole side of his head was caved in. Somebody murdered him. Don't go down there, Molly."

Chapter XX

Molly left Nate Stiles talking to himself and ran to Benson's. She fought herself to control the cold fear that was now near panic. She was breathless when she reached Benson's and could scarcely calm herself long enough to tell the livery boy she wanted a saddle horse.

While the horse was being saddled and bridled, Molly stood just inside the runway of the stable and watched the street. She could see part of the crowd in front of the Silver Dollar, but she could not see Standifer.

Molly rode out of town on the westbound road, feeling Standifer's presence as she had in her nightmare of the faceless man who threatened to kill her. She knew she had to find Charley Castle. She kicked her horse to a fast trot.

It was past sundown. Molly looked at the pale blue sky. While she knew only that Charley Castle's mine was on the fringe of the JD Ranch, she thought she could find it within the next hour. There was that much good light left.

Molly had ridden only a mile when she heard a horse crash out of the trees and brush beside the road. She saw the man with his Stetson pulled low on his face come charging out of the screen of trees, and fear knotted her stomach as she kicked the horse again. *He knew I would come this way!*

The chase was a short one. Standifer's horse was fast. He galloped up tight to Molly's side, grabbed her horse's reins, and hauled both animals down to a walk. Standifer turned off the road and led Molly's horse through a stand of lodgepole pines. When they reached a meadow fifty yards away, he stopped the horses.

"Climb down," Standifer said.

Molly hesitated, only now remembering the derringer in her handbag. It was too late.

Angered by her hesitation, Standifer rode close and grabbed Molly by the arm. He yanked her out of the saddle like a rag doll. Pain blasted through Molly's hip as she fell to the grassy earth. Tears burst from her eyes.

Luke Standifer took the handbag that was on the saddle horn of Molly's horse. He threw some of the contents out, sneering suddenly as he discovered Molly's derringer. He snatched it out and shoved the weapon into his trouser pocket. Then he brought out Molly's Fenton badge and identification card.

"Molly Owens, Fenton Investigator," Standifer read. "I figured you was a Fenton or a Pinkerton, one." He looked at Molly. "You was hired by Bess Tanner to pin that killing on me, wasn't you?"

Molly raised up and shook her head. "No, you're wrong—"

"The hell I am," Standifer said angrily. He drew out his revolver and aimed it down at Molly. "You played me for the fool."

Molly rolled off her sore hip and looked up at Standifer. "No, I didn't. You did that all by yourself."

Standifer's brow knotted, then he smiled. "Climb back up on that horse, Molly Owens. We're going for a ride."

Molly made no move to get up. Still smiling, Standifer holstered his revolver and dismounted. He grabbed Molly's wrist and jerked her to her feet. When Molly tried to pull back, Standifer backhanded her across the face, hard.

Before her consciousness slipped away, Molly saw dark, fluid shapes swim past her vision, then she was lifted up into the air and into darkness.

At first Molly thought the ground was moving beneath her,

but then she opened her eyes and saw she was on horse-back, her hands tied to the saddle horn, her feet tied to the stirrups. Standifer was in front, leading her horse. Ute Mountain loomed ahead.

Standifer rode around the base of the mountain, then angled up the side. The climb was steep and the horses took it slowly. It was nearly dark when they reached a narrow shelf high on the mountainside. The shelf was open along the front, but back against the mountain was a long clump of aspen trees. Standifer rode close to them and stopped. Molly heard the aspen leaves clattering together in the evening breeze.

Standifer dismounted and came back to her horse. He untied her numb feet and hands and lifted her off the saddle to the ground. Her ankles buckled and pain shot through her bruised hip. Standifer caught her and led her toward the aspen grove.

Molly was dizzy and the thought that came to her seemed to be from far away and had little significance for her: *He will kill me now.*

In the trees Molly felt a new coolness. There was a new smell in the air. The smell was damp and somewhat musty. Then a round, dark shape appeared in front of her, and Molly tried to plant her feet. Standifer shoved her ahead.

Molly sprawled onto the cool dirt floor of a cave. She raised up and looked around, but could see nothing. A match flared behind her. She looked back and glimpsed Standifer's shadowy face. Molly heard the *clink* of a chain, then Standifer threw the match aside. It fell to floor of the cave like a small, yellow comet, and went out.

Standifer grasped Molly's ankle. She tried in vain to pull away. Then she tried to kick him with her free leg, but could not. Cold steel clamped over her ankle, and the scream that came to her throat was only a dry sound that rasped out into the heavy darkness.

"Holler all you want," Standifer said. "Nobody'll hear you. Nobody but dead injuns."

Molly rolled over and sat up. She moved until her weight

was off her one painful hip. Standifer was a shadow, outlined by the pale evening light that came in through the mouth of the cave. Again Molly realized she was reliving her nightmare. She could not escape from this faceless man. She reached to her ankle. She felt a leg iron attached to a chain.

"I had plans for you," Standifer said in the darkness. "Good plans for you and me. But you played me for the fool. You was lying to me all along."

Molly cleared her throat. She barely recognized her own voice when she said, "Bess Tanner didn't hire me. I came here on my own. You must believe me."

Standifer said, "That's another lie."

"No," Molly said, "I can prove it."

"How?" Standifer asked.

"My last name is Owens," she said.

After a pause Standifer said, "So what?"

"Don't you remember the name of that young cowboy you murdered?" Molly asked. Her voice was shrill and rasping.

"Hell, no," Standifer said. "What are you getting at?"

Molly felt tears flood into her eyes. He didn't even know the name of the man he killed.

"His name was Owens," Molly said, "Chick Owens."

Standifer asked slowly, "You a relation?"

"He was my brother," Molly said.

Standifer was silent for a moment. "Well, if you came here to even the score, why didn't you just shoot me down? You had plenty of chances."

"If I had," Molly said, "I'd be no better than you."

Standifer grasped her leg and squeezed. "What are you saying?"

"I'm saying that Bess Tanner didn't hire me," Molly said.

"She knows you're here," Standifer said.

"That's all she knows," Molly said. "She can't hurt you."

"We'll see," Standifer said.

"Leave her alone," Molly said.

Standifer laughed dryly. "You're in a funny place to be telling me what to do."

Molly said, "Are you going to kill me like you killed Cinnamon Sam?"

Standifer was slow in answering. Molly heard him breathing in the darkness like a large animal. Then he said:

"Who's your partner?"

"What partner?" Molly said.

"I have had dealings with you Fentons before," Standifer said. "I know you work in pairs. Who are you working with?"

Molly said nothing. She tried to think of a way to use this to her advantage. "He knows as much about you as I do."

"I figured that," Standifer said. "If I knew who he was, I might be able to steer him out of town so he wouldn't get hurt."

"If you knew who he was, you'd kill him," Molly said. "Or you'd try to pin the murder of Cinnamon Sam on him."

Standifer laughed again. "We think alike. I'm going to have to find somebody to pin it on. A town the size of Liberty is going to be a hard place for a Fenton man to hide. I believe I can flush him out."

Molly heard and then saw him stand. His voice came from above when he said, "I ain't got time for you now. I have to get back to town. But your time is coming, woman. I aim to make you pay for what you done to me. You played me for the fool, and you're going to regret it."

Molly caught a glimpse of Standifer as he ducked through the mouth of the cave, then he was gone. She heard him ride away. From the sounds of the horses, she knew he had taken hers, too.

Molly turned on her good hip. Pain seeped through her other hip. She rubbed it. She was certain nothing was broken. She guessed she had a deep bruise. The numbness was out of her ankles and wrists now. She touched her cheek lightly where Standifer had backhanded her. The skin was broken below her cheekbone.

Even though there was no light in the cave now, Molly sensed the size of the place. It felt as large as a room in a house. Standifer had stood to his full height. Molly leaned forward and touched her ankle. She ran her fingers over the leg iron and chain. She had seen men shackled in leg irons many times. The one thing she knew about them was that they were escape-proof.

Molly touched the chain. She pulled until it drew tight, then crawled, following the chain to its end. It was about four feet long and was attached to a small metal ring. The bottom of the ring was flush with the dirt floor of the cave.

Molly dug her fingers around the base of the ring. In dismay she realized the ring was welded to the top of an iron bar. This bar had been driven deep into the dirt. Molly pulled on the chain, but could not budge it.

Again Molly ran her fingers along the length of the chain, feeling each link. If there was a weak one, she was unable to find it.

In sudden desperation Molly yanked on the chain with all her might. Sweat broke out of her face. Her ears pounded. Her grip loosened and she fell back, remembering her nightmare. Escape was impossible.

That evening Charley Castle found Justin Dundee on his front porch, smoking an afterdinner cigar. The old rancher did not stand when Charley Castle stopped his ore wagon at the tie post.

Justin Dundee took his cigar from his mouth. "Get out of here, Tucker."

"I have something to tell you, Mr. Dundee."

"You don't know one damned thing I need to hear," Dundee said.

"I believe I do," Charley Castle said. "I've struck a rich deposit of gold on that quarter section. Did Standifer tell you that?"

Dundee did not answer.

"Anyhow," Charley Castle went on, "Standifer has big plans for that land."

"What kind of plans?" Dundee asked tonelessly.

"After the gold deposit plays out," Charley Castle said, "he plans to sell off claims to prospectors."

Dundee got to his feet. "I thought Standifer sold out to that fat speculator in town."

"He'll buy it back," Charley Castle said.

"That speculator is a fool," Dundee said, "but he ain't fool enough to sell out now."

"He doesn't know about the gold strike," Charley Castle said. "Standifer thinks he can get back the land before Goodwin finds out."

"The hell," Dundee said. "He probably can."

"I thought you'd want to know," Charley Castle said.

"You say Standifer aims to sell off that land piece by piece?" Justin Dundee asked.

"By the square foot, I'd say," Charley Castle said.

The remark rubbed salt into an open wound. Justin Dundee walked to the end of the porch. He looked in the direction of the quarter section and swore. Then he turned back and faced Charley Castle.

"What's your angle, Tucker?"

"I don't have one," Charley Castle said. "I figure on making a fair piece of money off that little mine. When it plays out, I'll move on. I'd take no pleasure in seeing a fine ranch like yours overrun with gold seekers. I've seen it happen before, and it's not a pretty thing. The only way you'll be able to stop men with gold fever is to hire an army to ride your fences. You'll have a war here if Standifer has his way."

Justin Dundee shook his head at this thought. He said in a low voice, "Standifer will have to be stopped."

Charley Castle said, "The law might do it for you, Mr. Dundee."

"What do you mean?" Dundee asked.

"Everybody knows the kind of man Standifer is," Charley Castle said. "He's killed plenty of good men. If anybody testified against him, anybody who knew something about a killing, Standifer would be out of business."

Dundee turned away. As an afterthought, he said, "I don't know what you're driving at, Tucker."

But Charley Castle knew better. Justin Dundee's lined face looked haggard now as he wrestled with the problem in his mind. Charley Castle turned the wagon and drove down the ranch road toward the main road to town. The next step was to have Molly pay a visit to Dundee.

Chapter XXI

By nightfall Charley Castle had finished a late supper and returned to the Liberty Hotel. Molly was not in her room. He wondered where she could be and was tempted to ask Nate Stiles. But at last he left the hotel, thinking he should not tip his hand yet. He crossed the street and walked down the boardwalk to the Silver Dollar Saloon. The gaming tables and roulette wheel were going full tilt now.

Melvin Goodwin stood at the bar, bleary-eyed. When he recognized Charley Castle, he yelled at him over the din of the crowd. When Charley Castle joined the speculator, he spoke in a low voice that reeked of whiskey:

"How's that mine of yours, Mr. Tucker? Have you struck ore?"

"Not enough to brag about," Charley Castle said.

Goodwin smiled as though a secret thought of his had been confirmed. "Well, it's a gamble like you said. I swung a big deal today. It's supposed to be confidential, but I figure you have a right to know about it."

"What kind of deal?"

Goodwin looked around to be sure no one was close enough to overhear him. As usual, Charley Castle noticed, the other men in the saloon were giving Melvin Goodwin plenty of room.

"I traded off that quarter section to Luke Standifer. You see, I know something about him. He has a weakness for mines. I happen to know he's put money into them before. Well, I let it drop that a real geologist was working on this mine. And now today he looked me up and told me he was ready to trade me out of that quarter section. I got a prime section of railroad land up north out of the deal, Mr. Tucker."

"It sounds to me like you're gambling, too, Mr. Goodwin," Charley Castle said.

Goodwin's loose facial features took on an expression of surprise. "How's that?"

"You're gambling the railroad will run a line past Liberty in our lifetime," Charley Castle said.

Goodwin laughed. "Why, that's no gamble, Mr. Tucker. The railroad's coming, all right. You can bank on that." Goodwin drank, then offered the final proof for his conviction. "Things wouldn't have gone this far, Mr. Tucker, if the railroad wasn't planning to run a line past Liberty. No, sir."

Goodwin turned back to the bar and waved at the bartender for a refill. The bartender was unsmiling and appeared morose. He deliberately refilled Goodwin's glass, then saw Charley Castle for the first time.

"Drink, Mr. Tucker?"

"Rye," Charley Castle said. After the bartender poured the drink and left, Charley Castle observed that he looked as if he had lost his best friend.

"Haven't you heard?" Goodwin asked.

"Heard what?"

"He did lose his best friend," Goodwin said. "Somebody caved in Cinnamon Sam's head this afternoon. Right upstairs here. Somebody murdered him. He looked awful, I can tell you. I wish I hadn't looked at him."

"Murdered?" Charley Castle said.

Goodwin nodded. "It couldn't have been an accident. Nobody can figure it. Cinnamon Sam never had any money. He was nothing but a swamper. I hope Standifer finds out who did it."

Charley Castle left the saloon and rushed back to the hotel. He tapped on Molly's door. This time when there was no answer, he brought out his ring of skeleton keys. He opened the door and entered the room.

Charley Castle lighted a lamp and felt an immediate sense

of relief. The room was empty. Until then he feared he might find Molly's body here, as Cinnamon Sam's had been found. Charley Castle had no doubt that Standifer had somehow learned of Cinnamon Sam's betrayal and killed him for it. The question was, had Molly learned of the killing in time to get away?

After a quick search of the room, Charley Castle determined that Molly's handbag and riding outfit were missing. Some clothes lay in a pile on the floor. Perhaps Molly had changed there and had not picked the clothes up because she had left in a hurry. Charley Castle tried to take comfort in the fact there was nothing in the room to indicate that Molly had left here against her will.

Downstairs Charley Castle told Nate Stiles that he wanted to speak to Miss Castle about some mining property on the Circle 7 Ranch. She was a friend of the ranch owner and he had been anxious to talk to her, but now he could not find her. Nate Stiles said that she had left town early this evening. He suggested she might have gone to the Circle 7 Ranch.

Charley Castle returned to his room. He hoped Nate Stiles was right.

Molly woke at dawn. She was thirsty and stiff from sleeping on the cold, hard floor of the cave. She sat up. Her hip was not as painful as it had been last night, but the leg was stiff now. She touched her cheek where Standifer had hit her. A scab was there now.

Molly could not remember sleeping, but she knew she must have, off and on. She did remember peering into the darkness, fearing that a wolf or a bear would come into the cave.

The cave faced east. At sunup it was filled with light and grew warm. The cave was even larger than she had imagined it to be. It was twice the size of a large room in a house. The opening was large enough to drive a buggy through.

Now by daylight Molly examined the leg iron and chain that held her. She had been right about them last night. The chain was strong. And there was no escaping the leg iron short of cutting one's foot off. Even if Molly had a way of doing that, she knew she couldn't.

Again Molly looked around the cave. At the rear it narrowed and sloped down to the floor. Molly shuddered when she saw a scattering of bones there. They were human remains. Along with them were several stone tools. Then as Molly looked at the sides of the cave, she saw that narrow ledges had been carved out. These were man-made.

Molly got to her feet, keeping her weight off her sore leg. When she was at a level to see the ledges, she remembered what Bess Tanner had told her about Ute Mountain.

Skeletons were laid out on the ledges. Some were covered by rotting blankets; others were covered only by stiffened human flesh. And as Molly turned and looked at the corpses that encircled her, she saw that many were armed with bows and arrows and stone tomahawks decorated with feathers.

Molly sank to her knees. Though she was horrified at the sight of the corpses, an idea had come to her. She needed a weapon. Plenty were here if she could reach them.

Molly saw a tomahawk at the back of the cave. She crawled toward it until the chain went tight, then stretched out the full length of her body. But even as she did so, she knew the chain was too short. And she knew that tomahawk was closer than any of the other weapons. She stretched out and pulled against the chain even though she knew the effort was futile.

Surprisingly, her fingers plunged into soft dirt. The ground where she had slept was packed hard as stone. She dug her fingers into the dirt and touched fine cloth.

Her first thought was that this could not have been made by Indians. She grasped the silky cloth and pulled. Even as she sat up and saw the cloth's bright red color, Molly felt sickened.

The dress was torn across the front. Molly spread it out before her and pulled it together where it was ripped. White initials were sewn across the front: JH.

Molly knew Jennifer Hayes was buried here, or nearby. There could be no doubt of it. And Molly had little doubt what the young woman had endured before her death.

Frantically, Molly looked at the chain again. She followed

it link by link to the metal ring. She scraped her fingers on the hard dirt there. She broke a fingernail to the quick, and jerked her hand back in pain.

The pain brought Molly to her senses. She could never dig out that iron bar with her bare hands. She needed a tool. Among those corpses, there probably was a digging tool. But she could not reach them.

As Molly calmed herself and gathered her thoughts, she ran her hand along her sore hip. Her hand brushed the buttoned pocket of her riding skirt. The objects she felt there brought back a sad memory, yet filled her with excitement, too. She remembered sorting through Chick's belongings. She had decided to keep only two: the pocket watch and the Barlow knife.

Molly unbuttoned the pocket and brought out the knife. She opened the single blade. It was four inches long, and sharp. Molly looked at it as it gleamed in the sunlight, thinking, *Chick is helping me now.*

Molly jabbed the knife into the dirt around the iron bar that had been driven into the cave's floor. The blade went in only half an inch. She jabbed repeatedly into a small area, then brushed the dirt away. She had made a shallow hole beside the iron ring that was welded to the iron bar. This was going to be slow and tedious.

Molly had no idea how long the iron bar was. She tried not to think about it. She had to concentrate on digging. Another thing she tried not to think about was how much time she had before Standifer would return.

Chapter XXII

At dawn Charley Castle left Liberty, driving his ore wagon out of town on the westbound road. By sunup he had driven past the JD Ranch road and found the Circle 7 road.

He followed the rutted, winding road through the low hills

until he crested the last grassy hill before reaching Ute Mountain. The rich valley below held the log house and outbuildings of the Circle 7 Ranch. Molly had described this ranch to Charley Castle, and now he saw she had not exaggerated. This was a fine ranch.

As he drove toward the house, Charley Castle saw a big woman crossing the yard on her way to a slab shed beside the corral. With her was a bearded, shaggy man. The two stopped to watch Charley Castle approach. The woman wore overalls, boots, and a man's shirt. And as he drove closer he saw that the shaggy man's head was covered with green leaves.

The big woman gestured to the shaggy man. He walked on to the shed, casting a glance back at Charley Castle as the ore wagon came to a halt in front of the house. The woman crossed the yard and greeted him.

"What can I do for you, mister?" she asked, casting a skeptical look at the big-wheeled wagon.

"My name is Charles Tucker," Charley Castle said. "I believe you are Bess Tanner."

"Are we acquainted?" Bess asked.

"No, we aren't," Charley Castle said. "But we have a mutual friend: Molly Castle."

Now Bess's eyes narrowed with suspicion. "Well, I still don't know why you're here, Mr. Tucker."

"I'm looking for Molly."

"I don't know where she is," Bess said. "She ain't here."

Charley Castle did not know if Bess was telling the truth or not. She would certainly lie to protect Molly. He said, "I'm working on the Luke Standifer case with Molly."

"She never told me nothing—" Bess stopped herself, then added, "about any such thing."

"You'll have to take my word for it," Charley Castle said. "The important thing now is that I find her."

"Well, I can't help you," Bess said. "You might as well ride on back the way you came."

"I'll leave if you order me off your place," Charley Castle said, "but I think you ought to hear me out. Molly's real name is Molly Owens. She's gathering evidence against Luke Standifer because she believes he murdered her brother. Her brother, Chick, was working for you when he was killed."

Charley Castle watched the woman's face as he spoke. She was surprised at what he knew. He went on, "Now Molly's disappeared. The more time it takes me to find her, the less chance there is of finding her alive."

"What do you mean?" Bess asked. Then she said, "Mr. Tucker, you step down off that big wagon and come inside. I want to hear about this over coffee."

In the kitchen Charley Castle sat at the round oak dining table and told her about the murder of Cinnamon Sam. Now Standifer must know that it was Molly who had forced Cinnamon Sam to talk about Chick's death. That was the only reasonable explanation for Molly's disappearance.

"You think she heard about that swamper's murder and left town," Bess said.

Charley Castle nodded. "I thought she'd come here."

Bess shook her head. "She ain't here. That's the truth." Bess considered the meaning of this, and asked, "You think Standifer caught her?"

Charley Castle nodded.

"I knew she shouldn't have tried to fool that killer," Bess said. "I just knew it."

For the last several minutes, Charley Castle had been aware that someone was lurking around the screen door of the kitchen. Bess had been too involved in the conversation to notice. Charley Castle caught her eye and jerked his head toward the door.

"Barney," Bess called over her shoulder, "you either get in here where I can see you, or go back to the shed. You ain't supposed to spy on folks." In a lower voice, she said to Charley Castle, "You'll have to pardon Barney. Since Chick was killed, he's decided it's up to him to look out for me."

The back door slowly opened. Barney came inside, but stayed near the door. Keeping his leaf-covered head bowed, Barney laced his thick fingers together. He said, "You was talking about Molly. What's wrong?"

"If you was spying," Bess said impatiently, "you know as

much as we do." To Charley Castle, she said, "This here is Barney Barnes. Barney, this gentleman is Mr. Charles Tucker."

"He ain't no gentleman," Barney said dully. "I don't like him."

"Barney!" Bess exclaimed. "That's no way to talk. Mr. Tucker's a guest."

"I seen him setting off dynamite over on the JD," Barney said. "He's a miner or something. And I seen him riding with Standifer."

Now Bess looked at Charley Castle. "What about this, Mr. Tucker?"

Charley Castle knew it would be hard enough to fool a woman like Bess. She was an open, direct sort of woman who could probably sense deviousness in others. But he worried more about Barney. In his years of experience with working various games on street corners and with encountering a few hermits and wild-eyed prospectors in mining camps, Charley Castle had learned a hard lesson: You can con a smart man or a stupid man, but you can't con a crazy man. Barney was one of these. Charley Castle realized that now he would have to resort to the truth.

"I need your help in finding Molly," he said. "I'll tell you how all this came about."

By late morning Molly had opened blisters in the palms of her hands from repeatedly jabbing the Barlow knife into the hard dirt. But in her desperation to free herself, she was only vaguely aware of the pain. For she knew that if she could not use the knife to escape, she would have to face Standifer with it.

When she had dug down nearly a foot all around the iron bar, Molly grasped it and put her weight against it. She could get a firm grip on the bar now, but as she shoved and pulled she saw could not budge it. That meant the bar was very long, perhaps four feet or more in length.

Molly began digging with the knife again. The end of the blade was no longer a point; it was rounded. And soon Molly struck a small stone. She found others, and the deeper she dug, the larger they were. Some of the stones could be pried out, but others required much extra digging before they could be loosened. The hole around the iron bar was growing wider, but scarcely deeper. And when she tried to pry out a stone the size of an apple, the blade broke.

Molly looked at the knife in disbelief. Less than half the blade remained. She felt tears of frustration well up in her eyes, yet she knew she must hold them back. The knife could still be used as a digging tool, but the work would go even slower now. Worse, Molly thought as she plunged the knife into the rocky soil again, if Standifer returned before she could free herself, the broken knife would not be much of a weapon.

During the telling, Barney stood by the kitchen door, listening intently but showing little expression in his face. Bess, however, was surprised. She was amazed at learning about the relationship between Standifer and Dundee.

"I was wrong about Justin," she said. "I wonder what made him throw in with a man like Standifer."

"Maybe he didn't want to," Charley Castle said. What he did not say was that his plan to put Standifer and Dundee at odds was jeopardized by Molly's disappearance. He doubted now that his plan could be carried through the way he had intended.

Bess said, "Do you reckon Molly might have gone into hiding in the Rockwell House?"

Charley Castle doubted it. He recalled that Nate Stiles had seen her leave town on the westbound road. Somewhere between the edge of town and the Circle 7 Ranch, he said, Molly had run into trouble.

"You mean Luke Standifer," Bess said.

Charley Castle nodded.

"But how can we help? Barney and me can't comb all the country between here and town. Where do we start?"

"We start by believing Molly has been kidnaped. Do you

know of some places between here and town where she might
be held?"

Bess nodded thoughtfully. "I reckon so. We can sure give
it a try. What do you aim to do?"

"I'll go back to the mine," Charley Castle said. "There is a
slim chance that Molly found it and decided to hole up
there. If I don't find her, I'll go back to town. I want to know
what Standifer is doing. I hope he's busy investigating the
murder of Cinnamon Sam."

"That's a laugh, ain't it?" Bess said.

Charley Castle left the Circle 7 Ranch and drove his ore
wagon back to the mine. The name Standifer had chosen for
the mine was more ironic now than ever. A careful search
of the ground around the tunnel showed no fresh sign of a
horse or a woman. Molly was not at the Molly Mine.

Late in the morning Charley Castle left his wagon and
mule team at Benson's. He asked the livery boy if he recalled
renting a saddle horse to a woman last evening. The boy
did; the woman had been a good customer lately. Charley
Castle asked if the horse had been returned. The boy shook
his head slowly. Charley Castle left the boy before he could
ask the reason for the inquiry.

Crossing the street, he walked past the empty marshal's
office. He recrossed Main and walked down the boardwalk
toward the Silver Dollar Saloon. He realized it was noon because the train was in. A thick column of dark smoke boiled
up behind the depot building that marked the end of Main
Street. Liberty's idlers, having seen the train safely in and observed and commented on its condition, were returning to
their places in the shade along Main, or inside the Silver
Dollar Saloon where some of the travelers might come with
news from Denver.

Inside the Silver Dollar, Charley Castle sensed a new mood.
All the men were subdued, listening to two who were carrying valises. It was apparent they had just got off the train, and
they had brought bad news. Melvin Goodwin sat alone at a
table with his hands covering his face.

Charley Castle picked up enough of the talk to know that the owners of the railroad had gone bankrupt. The line would not go past Liberty in the foreseeable future.

Standifer was not in the saloon. Charley Castle walked back up Main, stopping at the cafe that he knew he frequented. And he saw him through the window. The marshal sat at a table with another man. Charley Castle went inside.

Standifer looked up at Charley Castle. He hesitated, then waved for him to come over. The second man had his back to Charley Castle, and when Standifer prepared to introduce him, the man turned in his chair. Charley Castle knew him. He was Clarence Hoffman.

Chapter XXIII

Charley Castle had a bad moment after Clarence Hoffman turned in his chair and put his hand out to shake. But when their eyes met, Charley Castle saw no recognition in Hoffman's. His handshake was perfunctory and brief. He turned and spoke to Standifer.

"I hope we can work together in the next few days, Marshal. I can help you, and maybe you can help me."

Standifer nodded. "Maybe so, Mr. Hoffman."

Clarence Hoffman shoved his chair back and stood. "I'm obliged to you for telling me what you know about the woman. I'll go to work on tracking her down."

Charley Castle answered the big man's nod as he walked past him on the way to the door. He stopped at the cash register there and paid for his coffee. Charley Castle sat down in the chair Hoffman left, but turned it enough so that he could see the departing Fenton investigator. Standifer watched him, too. At the door, Hoffman paused as though thinking of something, then after a last glance at the table he had left, he departed.

"Friend of yours?" Charley Castle asked.

"Not hardly," Standifer said. "He's a goddamn Fenton. How's things going at the mine?"

Since Charley Castle was certain no one had been at the mine that morning, he felt free to let Standifer assume he had put in a morning's work. He said the vein was holding up. The ore he had brought out was still the same high-grade gold that Standifer had seen.

"That's what I like to hear," Standifer said. He studied Charley Castle, then asked, "What are you doing with the ore you've brought out of the tunnel so far?"

"It's out at the mine," Charley Castle said. "So far it hasn't amounted to more than a few hundred dollars. You trust me, don't you, Standifer?"

"Why, sure, I trust you," Standifer said. "It's other folks I don't trust. There's a lot of talk in this town about you working a mine near the JD. I reckon Goodwin's been shooting his mouth off. Somebody might go out there and do some night work. Get what I mean?"

Charley Castle nodded. "What do you think we ought to do about it?"

"I'm afraid you ain't going to like my idea," Standifer said. "I think you ought to start living out there."

"You're right," Charley Castle said. "I don't much like it."

"Later on I can spell you," Standifer said. "Right now I have to stick with the marshaling job. Folks are jumping down my throat about the killing of Cinnamon Sam. Everybody's scared of a murderer being on the loose."

Charley Castle marveled at the detached coolness of the man. He was actually going through the motions of searching for a killer. Charley Castle said, "You aim to quit this job?"

Standifer nodded. "But keep it under your hat. This town depends on me for law and order. If folks knew I was leaving, they'd get scared."

"What are you going to do?" Charley Castle asked.

"I'll invest the money I make off the mine in a horse ranch," Standifer said.

"Who's the woman named Molly?" Charley Castle asked.

As Charley Castle hoped, the question caught Standifer off guard. For a moment he showed surprise, then anger. "Why are you asking, Tucker?"

"You named the mine Molly," Charley Castle said easily. "There's a woman by that name in the Liberty Hotel."

"So?"

"I wondered if this was the woman you knew," Charley Castle said. "I've talked to her a few times. She's a friend of the woman who owns the Circle 7 Ranch. I believe there might be some good mining property over there. I wanted to talk to her about meeting the ranch owner, but now I can't find her. Molly seems to have disappeared."

"I wouldn't know about that woman," Standifer said. He leaned close and spoke in a low voice: "Tucker, after our mine is played out. I don't give a damn what you do or who you talk to. But right now you stick to our business." He leaned back in his chair and added, "You start living out at the mine. You can camp under that wagon of yours."

"Why, sure, I will," Charley Castle said. "I'll go back to the hotel and get my gear."

"We understand each other, Tucker," he said, satisfied. "I've got a lot on my mind. I don't want to have to be worrying over the mine." Standifer looked down at the food left on his plate. He picked up the fork, then dropped it. He shoved back his chair and stood, jamming his Stetson on his head.

"Maybe I'll ride out and see you this afternoon, Tucker," Standifer said.

Charley Castle watched the marshal pay for his meal and leave the cafe. He went to the window and watched. Standifer was headed for Benson's, but was stopped on the way by two men who engaged him in conversation.

Charley Castle left the cafe and cut across the street. Now was the time to follow Standifer, but he wanted to get his revolver from his room.

For the first time since Charley Castle had come to Liberty, Nate Stiles was not in the lobby. Charley Castle took note of this, then went up the stairs two at a time and strode down the hall. The door to his room was standing open.

He stopped and listened. He thought he heard a man's rough breathing. Edging forward, he looked into the room. Nate Stiles was slumped in a chair in the middle of the room, bleeding from a cut across the side of his head. Charley Castle rushed in.

"Nate, what—"

Charley Castle was struck as soon as he entered the room. He lost his balance and went down, sliding up against Nate Stiles's feet. Charley Castle got on all fours, but he was kicked in the side. He rolled over, holding his middle. Clarence Hoffman stood over him.

"Get up, Castle."

Painfully, Charley Castle straightened out. He got to his knees and stood. As Hoffman came after him, he circled away. Sensing an easy victory, Hoffman was in no hurry to corner him in the small room.

"You left me in a fix in Denver, Castle. You and that woman. Now I aim to put you in a fix. I'm going to bust you to pieces. You'll beg me to kill you before I'm through."

Charley Castle had circled toward the door, but Hoffman cut him off.

"Where are you going?"

As Hoffman spoke, his guard dropped. Charley Castle's fist lashed out, flattening Hoffman's nose. Blood spurted from both nostrils. For a moment Clarence Hoffman looked surprised. Then he was enraged. He wiped blood away from his mouth, and charged.

Charley Castle sidestepped, but he could not escape the big man's open-armed grasp. He felt himself pulled off his feet. He was picked up and thrown to the floor like a doll. Hoffman stood over him, mopping his bleeding nose. He breathed raggedly through his mouth.

"Get up, Castle."

Charley Castle stood up, at once knowing the craziness of this fight, and the futility. He could not win, yet he must try.

Again Hoffman moved in. Charley Castle feinted with his left, then threw a straight punch with his right to Hoffman's heart. The punch was a solid one, but had little effect. He might as well have slugged an ox.

Hoffman backed Charley Castle against the dresser. Out of the corner of his eye, Charley Castle saw the ceramic water pitcher beside the small washbasin on top of the dresser. Before Hoffman could grab him again, Charley Castle snatched the pitcher by its handle.

Clarence Hoffman saw what was coming. He slugged wildly. Charley Castle felt a glancing blow on the side of his face as he slammed the pitcher down on Hoffman's head.

Another man might have been killed. But Clarence Hoffman was felled to his knees. He shook his head from side to side like a bull who had just run into a tree. He was more confused and angered than hurt.

Charley Castle stepped around him and lunged for the door. Hoffman grabbed his ankle. Charley Castle fell to the floor. Hoffman reached out and grasped Charley Castle's shirt front. Looking into the man's ruined face, Charley Castle realized he was fighting on instinct now. Charley Castle hit him in the throat. Hoffman gasped, but in the next moment slammed his fist into Charley Castle's jaw.

Charley Castle's last memory was of being struck again. His head snapped too far around on his neck, and everything became dark and warm.

Water dripping over his face woke him. He blinked and saw Clarence Hoffman. He held a glass of water tipped so that water hit Charley Castle's face. In his other hand he held a bottle of whiskey. The side of Hoffman's face was swollen and raw.

"Get up, Castle. Get up, damn you."

Charley Castle sat up. He wiped the water from his face. He realized he must not look much better than Hoffman.

Clarence Hoffman said, "You fight good for a little man."

"I'm glad I've earned your respect," Charley Castle said.

The sarcasm went past Hoffman. "I don't know what kind

of game you're working in this burg, Castle, but it's all over now. Where's the woman?" Hoffman took a drink from the whiskey bottle.

"What woman?" Charley Castle asked.

"Play dumb with me and I'll whup you some more," Clarence Hoffman said. "I'll tear your leg off and shove it down your throat."

"That sounds like a threat," Charley Castle said. He looked around and saw that Nate Stiles was gone. "Where's Nate?"

"I let the old buzzard go back downstairs," Clarence Hoffman said. "I sent him out to find Standifer, but he couldn't find him. Somebody said he rode out of town an hour ago. That old buzzard had better be telling the truth if he wants to go on living. I sent him out to buy me a bottle of whiskey, but that don't mean we're friends."

Hoffman drank from the bottle again, then took a swallow of water. "When I met you over in the cafe, I knowed there was something familiar about you. I couldn't place you. Then I came over here to the hotel because Standifer said a woman named Molly Castle was here. When I looked her up in the register, I seen Charles Tucker was in the next room. That's when it came to me who you was. What kind of game are you working in this burg, Castle?"

"Investment," Charley Castle said.

Clarence Hoffman laughed dryly. "That ain't likely. I figure you aim to get rich off the railroad like everybody else in this town. Hell, maybe you are the railroad. That's your kind of game."

Charley Castle had to admit that the idea was interesting.

Hoffman picked his big revolver off the bed and waved it at Charley Castle. "I'm through playing games, Castle. You tell me where the woman is, or I'll pistol-whip you. You think you're hurting now, wait until I get done with you. I'll ruin you for women, permanent."

"I don't know where she is," Charley Castle said.

"That ain't the answer I'm looking for," Clarence Hoffman said. He moved closer and started to swing the barrel at Charley Castle's face.

Charley Castle put out his arm to deflect the blow. At the same time he tried to move away. That was when he saw someone coming up behind Hoffman.

Clarence Hoffman must have heard or sensed something, too, for he half-turned. It was too late. Barney Barnes brought the barrel of his revolver down on Hoffman's battered head. He sank to his knees, then fell on his face. He lay still.

Behind Barney Barnes, Nate Stiles came into the room. He helped Charley Castle get to his feet.

"I'm sorry I couldn't help you sooner," Nate Stiles said. "That man pistol-whipped me. He hurt me bad."

"I know," Charley Castle said. "Thanks for bringing Barney."

"I never brung him," Nate Stiles said. "He came here looking for you. I told him what was going on up here."

"Thanks, Barney," Charley Castle said. He looked down at the prone figure of Clarence Hoffman. "It's a good thing you hit him a good one. He has a hard skull."

"Bess sent me to fetch you," Barney said. "We found Molly's horse. And we found some of her things in a meadow."

Charley Castle crossed the room and opened his bag. He brought out his revolver and shoulder holster. "You work fast," he said as he put on the holster.

"We've been hunting all day," Barney said.

"What time is it?" Charley Castle asked in surprise.

Barney had no idea. Time had little meaning for him.

Nate Stiles said, "It's almost four o'clock."

"I must have been out longer than I thought," Charley Castle said, moving to the door. "Let's go, Barney."

Charley Castle was tired and sore. Every breath came painfully from his bruised chest and ribs. Some ribs might be cracked from the kick Hoffman had given him.

At Benson's he yelled hoarsely for the livery boy to saddle a horse for him. The boy took a wide-eyed look at his battered face and blood-spattered shirt, then he turned and ran to the corral. Charley Castle stopped at the water trough. He plunged his head and arms into the cold water.

Chapter XXIV

Molly found that the broken knife blade was a poor digging tool, but was better for prying out stones than a whole one. The hole she had dug around the iron bar was wide, and by early afternoon it was nearly two feet deep.

She grasped the bar and pulled. It did not move. Exasperated, Molly began digging again. On one side of the bar she had struck a large rock. She had to leave it in place. She dug out smaller stones and scooped out dirt from the rest of the hole. Soon the hole was deeper on one side.

Molly put her weight against the bar. This time, instead of trying to pull the bar up, she worked it from side to side. The bar moved. Excitedly, Molly got to her knees and worked the bar forward and backward, then from side to side. When she stood and pulled, the bar came free.

Molly fell to her knees. She was exhausted and now her fatigue overcame her. Both hands were raw. Her mouth was dry as leather and her tongue was swollen and rough. She needed water, but as she crawled to the mouth of the cave, she realized she would have none. Outside she heard and then saw a horse.

Molly hurriedly crawled to the mouth of the cave, dragging the chain and bar behind her. She moved to the side of the opening and peered out. Standifer had dismounted and tied his horse to a small aspen tree. Now he turned and walked toward the cave.

Molly looked around anxiously. She needed a weapon. Then she realized she was bound to one. She picked up the iron bar. It was a heavy club now, almost four feet long. When Standifer came through the opening, she would swing the club, aiming for his Stetson-covered head.

But what if she missed? Perhaps she should swing the bar

crosswise, hoping to stun him. She would have time to strike him again. But would she even have the courage now to hit a man with the intention of killing him? Torn by doubts in these last seconds, Molly feared she would be frozen by her own indecision. And then she knew she would never know what her reaction would have been.

Standifer apparently saw Molly was not where she should have been. He stood in the opening of the cave, then backed out. He had seen or heard her, and knew she was not bound to the chain.

"Don't make me shoot you, woman."

Molly lowered the iron bar and stood pressed up against the wall of the cave. Her own breathing seemed loud, and she wondered if Standifer had heard it. She was trapped, yet she was safe, too. Standifer could not shoot her without coming in and showing himself. Molly could strike back.

"I don't want to have to shoot you," Standifer said. "I got something to tell you."

Molly tried to answer, but found she could not raise her voice above a dry whisper. In reply she waved the iron bar in the opening of the cave.

"There's a friend of yours in town," Standifer said. "Only he ain't much of a friend."

Molly thought he meant Charley Castle. Had he taken him prisoner?

"This here man came in on the train," Standifer went on. "He's hot to find you and have you arrested. You'd better be glad I took you out of town."

Molly asked hoarsely, "Who?"

"A man by the name of Hoffman," Standifer said. "I ought to bring him up here and let him go in after you. He says you're in with Castle. He thinks Charley Castle might be disguised as a speculator in Liberty."

Molly wondered how Hoffman could have learned she was in Liberty; then she remembered the telegram she had sent to the city marshal's office in Denver. Hoffman must have friends there.

Standifer said, "You'd better come out. I could block off this cave. You'll die of thirst."

That was better than what he had in mind, Molly thought. She thought she had heard an undercurrent of doubt in Standifer's voice. She knew she could not go another day without water. In a few hours she would probably faint. But could Standifer stay here that long? Molly believed not, and for a moment she thought she had the upper hand. At worst, this was a stalemate. Then Standifer said:

"I'll smoke you out of there, woman."

Charley Castle followed Barney out of town. On the outskirts of Liberty Barney cut north and followed a stream bed. Several new buildings had been built here in anticipation of the railroad increasing the town's growth in this direction. Once these structures of raw lumber had been symbols of hope and speculators' dreams. Now, empty and beginning to weather, they looked forlorn.

Barney rode north and then angled west at a fast trot. This gently rolling hill country had been bought by land speculators who believed the rail line must come this way. Here and there stakes could be seen, marking a man's investment.

Barney generally followed the small stream of clear water, cutting across country where the bed meandered. Then after riding several miles, they dropped into a ravine. The lone horse, wearing the same brand as Charley Castle's mount, was staked here.

Charley Castle followed Barney farther on. They found Bess at the stream. She was on foot, searching the moist bank. When she saw Barney and Charley Castle approaching, she said desperately:

"I can't find their tracks!"

Charley Castle rode close to her. Bess told him she had found two sets of tracks where the horses had left the stream, but she could not find where they had entered.

Charley Castle looked upstream, scanning the countryside. The stream came down from Ute Mountain, still several miles away. Maybe the horses had been brought down the stream bed not for a few yards, but for a few miles. A careful man would do that.

"Where did you find Molly's belongings?" Charley Castle asked.

"Barney found them." Bess said, pointing back to the forest of lodgepole pines that spilled off the mountainside and, from here, concealed the westbound road.

"Show me, " Charley Castle said.

Barney led them to the meadow beside the road. Scattered in the tall grasses were two handkerchiefs, a small mirror, and a lady's wallet. Charley Castle rode in a widening circle around the meadow. He found two sets of hoofprints leading off through the trees.

"This way," he said.

The tracks led to the base of Ute Mountain. Charley Castle looked up at the high, rugged mountain. He thought he knew what had happened. Standifer had captured Molly on the road. He had discovered her identity in the meadow back there. He had taken her somewhere up on the mountain, then had led the horses down the stream bed. In another day, two at most, all the tracks would be gone. Now in the rocks at the base of Ute Mountain, there were no tracks.

Bess asked the question that was on all their minds: "Do you think she's still alive?"

"If Standifer intended to kill her, he'd have done it back in the meadow," Charley Castle said, realizing he was trying to convince himself as much as anyone.

"Where would he have taken her?" Bess asked.

Barney said, "The spirits'll take care of her."

"What are you talking about, Barney," Bess said irritably.

"There's spirit caves up there," Barney said.

Bess looked at Charley Castle. "I wonder if she's in one."

Charley Castle nodded. He asked Barney, "How many caves are up there?"

Barney looked puzzled, as though he had been asked how many stars were in the sky. "Never counted 'em," he said.

"Let's pick an easy trail up the mountainside," Charley
Castle said. "Then show me the nearest cave." To Bess he
added, "I guess we'll look in all of them until we find something. I don't know what we'll find. Maybe you ought to ride
back to the ranch and wait for us."

"Not on your life," Bess said. "Lead out."

Barney rode ahead, letting his horse pick his way up the
mountain. He had not gone far when he looked back at Charley Castle and pointed to a boulder. The bottom edge of it
had been scraped by the shoe of a passing horse.

After half an hour of slow climbing, Charley Castle heard
Bess hiss at him. He looked back and saw her gesture up the
slope. Straight above them a cloud of smoke was lifting from
what appeared to be a ledge. Charley Castle asked Barney
if there was a cave up there. The shaggy man nodded.

Charley Castle was trying to decide which would be the
best way to approach the ledge when he heard a gunshot.

Molly heard a noise outside. She took a quick look and
saw Standifer drag a dead aspen tree up to the mouth of
the cave. The tree was twice the height of a man, but was only
six or eight inches in diameter. She heard him snap off the
tree's smaller branches, then she smelled smoke. Another
quick look outside and Molly saw that he was using the small
branches and other twigs to ignite the broken stump.

She was trapped. She knew if she tried to make a break for
freedom, Standifer would shoot her down. Remembering the
bows and arrows she had seen with the Indian corpses, Molly
wondered if they could be usable after the many years of lying
here in the cave.

Outside Molly recognized the sound of the aspen tree being
dragged across the ground. The noise grew louder, and then
the smoking stump of the aspen tree slid into the cave like a
fire-breathing dragon. Smoke billowed off the smoldering
stump.

Within seconds smoke was thick inside the cave. Molly's
eyes watered as she tried to remember where one of the bows

was. She would have to show herself to reach the nearest bow, but she knew she had to try. She hoped the smoke would screen her from Standifer's view.

Molly was wrong. As soon as she stepped away from the wall of the cave, Standifer fired. Molly jumped back. The bullet had grazed her side. She felt as though she had been touched by a branding iron.

To Charley Castle's surprise, Barney turned his horse and spurred the animal straight up the mountainside toward the haze of smoke.

"Come back!" Charley Castle yelled.

Barney ignored him. The strong horse lunged up the mountainside, pawing dirt and sending back a shower of stones. Barney had all he could handle to stay in the saddle and had not drawn his gun when he reached the shelf.

From below, Charley Castle saw the horse lunge ahead to level ground. In the next instant he heard a shot. The horse reared and squealed in fear. Barney tumbled backward out of the saddle and rolled down the mountainside.

Charley Castle leaped out of his saddle. He ran uphill and caught Barney. He groaned. Charley Castle turned him over and saw he was bleeding from a ragged hole high in his chest.

Bess came up the mountainside and knelt beside Barney. "My God."

"Do what you can for him," Charley Castle said, drawing his revolver from his shoulder holster.

"Be careful," Bess said.

Molly heard Standifer curse. Her first thought was that his horse had broken loose and run off. But then she realized the loud sounds of hoofs clattering on loose rocks were growing louder and closer. Someone else was here. She heard a gunshot and the frightened squeal of a horse.

Molly knelt down and looked outside the cave. Tears ran from her eyes and she was choking on the smoky air now, but she was able to see Standifer. He was backing toward her, as though he expected someone to come up the side of the mountain.

Molly saw her chance. She got to her feet and picked up the

iron bar. She wanted to run out of the cave and strike down Standifer, but as she lunged ahead, she found she could not run. Outside she staggered, choking and crying. As she came up behind Standifer and made a wild swing with the iron bar, she fell to the ground.

The heavy bar smashed against Standifer's leg. He cried out and dropped to his knees.

Molly looked up and saw his face stretched with pain. He pressed one hand against his injured leg and cursed. His other hand held his revolver. Standifer raised the Peacemaker now as he took aim at Molly's face.

"Standifer!"

Standifer jerked his head around and looked in the direction the voice had come. Charley Castle stood at the edge of the aspen grove, holding his small revolver in both hands before him.

"I hear you're hunting Charley Castle," he said. "You're looking at him."

Rage swept through Standifer as he realized how thoroughly he had been deceived. With great speed and surprising accuracy, he swung his gun around and fired.

The bullet whispered past Charley Castle's ear. Steadying his own revolver with both hands, he took deliberate aim and squeezed back on the trigger.

Standifer's head shook once, as though stung. Then from the darkening spot near his Adam's apple, crimson blood spurted. Standifer went down, face first, choking on his own blood. He gurgled loudly and his body was racked with spasms for several moments, then he grew quiet and he lay still.

Chapter XXV

Molly woke in her room in the Liberty Hotel. The curtains were drawn, but from her bed she could see it was light outside. The sun was shining. On the nightstand was a pitcher

of water and a glass. Molly sat up. She poured the glass full
of water, drank it and half of another.

She tried to get out of bed, but when she put weight on
her feet, pain shot through her bruised hip. The pain brought
back a flood of memories and half-memories that now seemed
like old dreams. She remembered being in the cave, discover-
ing Jennifer's torn dress, Luke Standifer being shot, and
Charley Castle holding her and telling her everything was all
right. Her ordeal was over.

Yet Molly sensed everything was not all right. Without
knowing why, she felt troubled. Presently the door opened.
Bess Tanner came in.

"Well, look who's awake," she said.

"Have I slept all day?" Molly asked.

"Going on two days," Bess said.

"Two!" Molly exclaimed.

"And the doctor wants you to stay in bed at least two more
days," Bess said.

Molly lay back on the bed. She could not imagine two
days had passed.

Bess sat on the edge of the bed. "Do you remember what
happened up on the mountain?"

Molly nodded. "But everything's hazy after Charley Castle
came for me. Were you there? I can't remember if I saw
you, or dreamed I saw you."

Bess told her how she and Barney and Charley Castle had
found the cave. Barney had been shot by Standifer. He was
seriously wounded, but today the doctor had assured Bess
he would recover. The bullet had passed through him without
causing damage that was fatal.

"Barney claims the spirits saved him," Bess said, smiling.
"He claims the spirits saved you, too."

Molly shook her head. "No, you saved me—you and Barney
and Charley Castle. Where is he?"

Bess did not answer Molly's question. Instead she went on
to tell of her meeting with Justin Dundee yesterday.

"I couldn't believe he was mixed up with Standifer until

Charley Castle told me what he knew about them. I reckon he wanted my ranch and would stop at nothing to get it. My own father was like that in his later years. I told Justin what I knew about him and Standifer."

"What did he say?" Molly asked.

Bess reflected for a moment. "Justin looks older now, you know. Age is catching him. And the last few days he's had trouble with prospectors trespassing on the JD. He's been up day and night running men off his land. Now that everyone knows the gold mine was a fraud, maybe he won't have so much trouble.

"Anyway, when I told Justin what I knew, he broke down and cried. He said he knew he was a victim of his own greed. And he told me what he knew about the murder of your brother. During the trial, Standifer talked to Justin in private and said he had a grudge against Chick. Well, Justin said Chick was all that stood between him and my ranch. Justin said he wished Chick was out of the picture, too.

"Now, according to Justin, that was all that was said. The next thing he knew, Standifer came out to the ranch and told him he had done the job Justin wanted. He had killed Chick. He wanted to be paid for his work. Justin got scared. Whether he liked it or not, he was an accomplice. So he agreed to turn over a prime quarter section of bottom land to Standifer. He thought the deal would be kept secret. Of course, it wasn't. Standifer sold the land to a speculator who had more money than brains. And then Charley Castle came along. You know the rest."

After a pause, Bess said, "There is one thing I want to know, Molly. Do you plan to bring charges against Justin? You know he withheld evidence that would have convicted Standifer."

"No," Molly said. "I won't bring charges against him. I'm not out for revenge."

Bess nodded. "That's what I hoped you'd say. Justin Dundee has been a strong man all of his life. Now he has to live with something he did during a moment of weakness."

Molly asked again, "Where is Charley Castle?"

Bess hesitated before answering. "You know that man's in love with you, don't you, Molly?"

Molly felt her face grow warm. She shrugged.

"I wouldn't be surprised to find out you're in love with him, too," Bess said. "He's a good man. That's why I hate to tell you."

"Tell me what?" Molly asked. She added recklessly, "That he left town? I'm not surprised." But she discovered she was hurt by the thought.

"Charley Castle didn't leave town," Bess said. "He's in jail."

"Why?" Molly exclaimed. "For shooting Luke Standifer?"

"I don't know why," Bess said. "All I know is what I heard. The county sheriff came in on yesterday's train. He slapped Charley Castle and a man named Hoffman in jail."

Molly sat up. She threw the covers back and tried to get out of bed. Bess protested. Molly stopped, but not because of Bess. Again as she put weight on her feet, pain blasted through her hip and tears came to her eyes. She lay back in bed, frustrated.

"Maybe the sheriff had a good reason for putting him in jail," Bess said. "There might be a warrant out for him."

Molly knew there was, but she didn't try to explain it to Bess. It simply was not right for a man like Charley Castle to be in jail. He was no criminal. If anyone was a criminal, it was Clarence Hoffman.

Bess stayed a while longer. She tried to chat with Molly about the many townspeople who had inquired about her ordeal. Molly was something of a local heroine now. But this conversation was one-sided. At last Bess stood, saying she had to see about taking Barney back to the ranch. She knew he wasn't happy about being in town.

"I'll try to come back tomorrow, Molly," Bess said, taking her hand. "You rest easy now, hear?"

Molly smiled. "Thank you, Bess. Thank you for everything."

Late in the afternoon Molly heard a knock on her door.

"Come in."

Nate Stiles hobbled into the room, carrying a yellow envelope in his hand. He pulled the straight-back chair up near the bed and sat down.

"How are you feeling?" he asked.

"I'm all right, Nate," Molly said. Seeing a long bandage on the side of his face, she asked what had happened to him.

Nate Stiles was glad to tell her in detail what had happened in the hotel room day before yesterday. Charley Castle had confronted Clarence Hoffman. The two men had fought. Hoffman would have killed Charley Castle if he and Barney hadn't put a stop to it.

Nate Stiles went on to tell of the group of men from town, naming each man, who went to the cave to recover the body of Luke Standifer. One was Liberty's blacksmith. When he saw the iron bar with the chain welded to it, he recalled making it for Standifer. The blacksmith remembered that was the day after the killing of Chick Owens, the very day Jennifer was supposed to have left town. Jennifer's dress was found inside the cave. The men found freshly turned soil near the back of the cave and went about the grim task of digging up the nude body that was buried there. It was Jennifer.

"I wonder how long Standifer kept her chained up in there," Nate Stiles said. He glanced at Molly and added quickly, "It ain't a good thing to think on, I reckon."

Now that he had told his story, and the stories he had heard, Molly was able to get a question in: "Why is Charley Castle in jail?"

"From what I hear," Nate Stiles said, scowling, "it's because of that no-good Hoffman. Hoffman's in jail because I signed a complaint against him, and Hoffman threatened to leave town with his prisoner, Charley Castle. Hoffman pistol-whupped me, like I told you. He's gonna regret it, though."

Nate Stiles looked at the envelope in his hand. "Oh, I plumb forgot. This here telegram came to you a while ago."

Molly tore open the yellow envelope. The telegram was from the Fenton office in New York City.

Operative Molly Owens:

I have personally received word of your present where-abouts from Operative Clarence Hoffman. He is very likely in Liberty by now. I received your wire from Denver. I am sad to learn of your recent loss in your family. I hope by now you have been able to resolve matters to your satisfaction.

Clarence Hoffman has accused you of a number of crimes and unprofessional behavior while in the commission of your last assignment. However, since your past record with us has been excellent, and Hoffman's has not, I am inclined to discount his indictment of you until I learn your side of the dispute. I hereby request that you send me a detailed account of your work with Clarence Hoffman and your contact with a notorious confidence man named Charles Castle.

Sincerely,
Horace J. Fenton

PS. For your information, I must tell you that the former mayor of Topeka, Kansas, who drew the original complaint against Charles Castle and who employed us to locate him, has been appointed to complete the term of a recently deceased United States Senator from the state of Kansas. His complaint was withdrawn when he left for Washington. For us, then, the case is closed. Terminate your pursuit of Charles Castle. I have notified Clarence Hoffman by wire and apprised him of the above information.

Horace J. Fenton

Molly said, "Look what civilization has come to now."

"What was that?" Nate Stiles asked.

"Nothing," Molly said. "Will you do me a favor, Nate?"

"You name it," he said.

"Tell that county sheriff I want to talk to him," Molly said. "He has a man in jail who doesn't belong there."

Nate Stiles grinned. "You wouldn't be talking about Charley Castle, would you?"

"I would," Molly said.

Molly watched the old cowboy leave the room. She read the telegram again. Then she lay back in bed, remembering the first time she saw Charley Castle. It was in Silverthorne. His glance had passed by her, returned for an instant, and Molly had felt the exciting sensation of being pulled toward the man, and in that instant she had known he was the man she had been looking for all of her life. Now when Charley Castle was released from jail, Molly would find out if she was the woman he had been looking for.